LOVE ME LIKE THAT

TaKisha Trenean

For The Lover In You...

CONTENTS

CHAPTER ONE

Sexy sounds of old school R&B resonated from the speakers as we danced chest to chest. Well, more like grinded into each other. Idris was slowly adding gasoline to the fire that was emerging inside of me. My body hummed with need as he kissed the side of my neck and spoke into my ear.

"Raven, baby, are you ready for me?"

He nipped my ear lobe then used is tongue to sooth the sting. Inside I was screaming, "Yes! Yes! Hell, yes I am ready!" Instead, I simply nodded and murmured.

"Mmm hmm. Tonight, was perfect."

"And it will only get better from here." Idris flashed me a mischievous grin before he scooped me up and carried me upstairs to my bedroom. The room was filled with candles and rose petals which gave it a romantic glow. *When did he do all of this?* He gently laid me down in the middle of the bed, and I sat back on my elbows while he painstakingly took his time to take off his clothes piece by piece. He was everything I'd imagined. Tall with muscles wrapped in smooth dark chocolate and that voice. Damn that voice had me pooling between my thighs. I was going to lick every part of this man. Idris pinned me with his gaze and crawled in between my legs. He eyed me like he was ready to pounce. Thankfully, I chose not to wear any panties with this dress. Idris made a sound with his mouth similar to the sound your grandmother would make when you did something wrong.

"You've been a bad girl Raven."

"Have I?" I played coy, eager to wrap my legs around this man.

"Yes, you have, but don't worry. I'll make sure the punishment fits the offense."

Before I could make a witty combat, he flattened his tongue on my swollen lips and went to work. The man's mouth was blessed. He licked, sucked, and fingered me until I felt that familiar tingle from my stomach down to my pelvis, and he had me screaming out in ecstasy.

"Ah yes! Yes! I'm coming Idris..."

A blaring alarm made my eyes pop open. My heart damn near exploded out of my chest; it scared me so bad. Idris seemed unbothered. He moaned and continued to enjoy his feast. I sat up and looked around the room to figure out where the ear-piercing sound was coming from.

"You don't hear that? Idris? Idris!" My vision became blurry and I blinked rapidly.

"MOMMY!"

"What? Wait, what?"

I sprang forward and scanned my room with alarm. My sleep hazed eyes eventually landed on my precocious six-year-old, but no Idris. She stood in front of my bed dressed in her school uniform. I patted my body to make sure that I was clothed, then tossed the covers up to look under them.

"Sade what are you...?"

"Your alarm won't stop ringing, Mommy. Are we going to be late again?" She crossed her arms and her brows furrowed. She examined me with worry then pressed the button to dismiss my alarm.

"Shit, shit, shit!" I chanted as I jumped out of bed and rushed through my routine of getting ready. I quickly applied product to my short-tapered cut. Slipping into a pair of tights and a sports bra, I threw on a light hoodie and grabbed a pair of sneakers. It was only September, but the weather was abnormally cool.

The weather reports predicted record lows this fall and winter. When I made it downstairs, Sade was sitting at the counter eating a bowl of cereal. She looked so much like her damn daddy with her caramel skin and golden hair. I rolled my eyes and looked around for my phone charger.

"Are you ready? Did you put your homework folder in your bag?" As I crossed the kitchen, I fluffed her box braids and kissed her on the cheek.

"Yep." Sade hopped down from the stool and placed her bowl and spoon in the dishwasher. I grabbed a bottle of orange juice, two gummy vitamins, and handed it to her. She skipped ahead of me to the door.

"Found your charger, Mommy." She dangled it in her hand and giggled.

"Oh, thank God for you, Baby Girl. What would Mommy do without you? Let's go and put that seat belt on tight."

Once we were both secured, I pulled out of the garage and took off towards Sade's school. Anita Baker's *Angel* was playing on the radio and Sade hummed along. It was one of the songs I use to sing to her as a baby and still do when she was having a bad day. Our eyes met in the rearview mirror and we both smiled. My phone rang through the Bluetooth and interrupted our song.

"Aww, man." Sade huffed and tossed her hands up.

"Hey, hey!"

"What up, Ray? Where's my baby girl?" Sade's face lit up upon hearing her father's voice. She was a daddy's girl and loved that man more than anything. Not too long ago his voice had the same effect on me.

"I'm right here daddy. Mommy's about to drop me off to school."

"School? I thought you two would be on the road… Did Mommy forget to pack?"

"Mommy is right here and can hear you. I had to work." My eyes rolled back and fluttered.

"Yeah, okay." He kissed his teeth and laughed.

"Do you need something Tariq?"

"Actually…" I knew that voice and he was going to say something to have me going against the promise I made to myself.

"Bye, T. I'll let Sade call you when I get to my dad's. Baby, tell your daddy bye."

"Love you, Baby Girl… and yo' crazy momma."

"She's not crazy. We love you too. Bye daddy." Although she defended me, she giggled hysterically like her and her damn daddy shared some inside joke about me. I ended the call before he could say anything else.

By the skin of my teeth, I got her to school just before the tardy bell rang. Before she exited the car, she leaned over, kissed me on the cheek, and wished me a good day. That little girl was my pride and joy. She was everything to me. Although she wasn't conceived under the most ideal circumstances, she was loved and doted on by both of her parents. Sade was very smart for her age. Her school wanted to test her to place her in a grade level that would challenge her, but I wanted my baby to be in a classroom with her peers. Placing her in a class with older kids would only isolate her. I made sure that she had weekend and after school activities that would challenge her. She attended this amazing STEM program after school and took music lessons on Saturdays. My parents made sure that their kids were well rounded, and I wanted the same for Sade with the exception that I allowed her to choose her activities.

Once out of the school speed zone I sped off towards my gym. It was more like a holistic wellness and fitness center and it was my pride and joy. Self-Love Wellness and Fitness Studio was the one thing, other than my daughter, that I had gotten right. The center contained rooms for spin classes, yoga, dance fitness, bootcamp, and a space for your typical workout equipment. There was also a meditation room, a sauna, and a massage room. The place was staffed by all women because we knew our bodies more than any man could, and I wanted women to feel comfortable coming to a gym to work out without worrying about being ogled at. I did the early morning meditations with my employees to set the tone for the day, so I could not be late.

I pulled up to the studio with ten minutes to spare. I greeted everyone with a warm smile as I took quick steps towards my office. It was one of my favorite places. I had my own shower, sauna, and meditation space that sometimes doubled as a home-work space for Sade. My phone alerted as I locked my purse in-side my safe.

Rayne: What time are you getting here? Please don't be late for dinner Raven.

Me: Hi to you to Raynnie Pooh! Once I pick Baby Girl up from school, we will be on our way.

Rayne: Seriously? You were supposed to help. You promise that I wouldn't have to deal with Rasheeda by myself. I thought Sade was staying home today.

When I didn't immediately respond she texted again.

Rayne: You're not even packed, are you?

Me: Now why would you think that?

Rayne: Girl bye! Just get here. Don't flake out and disappoint dad.

"He's not even your daddy," I mumbled to myself although I would never say that to my sister's face. My mom had two chil-dren before she married my father, but he always treated and loved them like they were his own, so it was like they had two dads. I am a daddy's girl myself and I'm selfish when it comes to him. He's my only dad, so I'm not afraid to say that I'd rather have him all to myself, but he was a good man and had plenty of love to give. Mom and Dad had been best friends since middle school and dated for a little while. At some point they went their separate ways romantically but remained friends. My mom was married to her first husband, Nelson, and pregnant with Rayne when she realized that she could not live without my dad, so she filed for divorce. Now we're all one big happy family, weirdly enough that included my sisters' father, Nelson.

Anyway, Rayne was right. I fell asleep without packing so I planned to head back home after meditation and the HIIT class I was covering today. Rayne was my sister, but we were so close in age that she was also my best friend. We knew everything about each other. She was a perfectionist and always made a big to do out of every celebration. There was no doubt in my mind that she was freaking out after learning that I wasn't on my way as planned. Rasheeda was the strict, no nonsense motherly type and obviously the oldest. She brought order to our lives. Daddy was a state senator, and we were celebrating his sixtieth birthday this weekend. My sisters had absolutely nothing to worry about. I would be there on time, no worries.

CHAPTER TWO

Liam

The sounds of a rapid gunfire and explosions going on inside of my apartment jolted me out of my slumber. I reached under my pillow and aimed my gun at the shadows. My chest heaved up and down as I struggled to regulate my breathing. Shivers took over my body, but my sheets were soaked with sweat. I exhaled a sigh of frustration. This was starting to take a toll on me. I sat up in the bed and wiped the sleep from my eyes. I planted my feet on the ground and cradled my head in my hands.

"Lord help me."

I fell on my knees and began to pray. I prayed until my body was calm and I had no more words. I prayed until my body stopped trembling and I felt grounded to this reality. My loft was no longer a warzone, it was my safe haven, my place of peace. The time was four in the morning and I needed to be up at five so there was no way I was going back to sleep. Plus, I was too amped up anyway. I trudged to the bathroom and took care of my hygiene. My reflection in the mirror looked spooked; I needed to shake this. I wasn't my best when my anxiety was high. I changed into some basketball shorts, a t-shirt, and my running shoes before grabbing my keys and heading out. I loved going out this time of morning. The quietest hour always seemed to be right before the city began to wake up. Running was something that helped calm me down and clear my mind. I focused on my pacing and my breathing while my feet pounded the pavement. My phone was strapped to my bicep and Jay-Z was playing through my ear pods. I felt my muscles began to loosen up and I felt lighter, like I was flying. With every exhale I released the tension in my body.

I turned towards the park to jog alongside the river. Being around bodies of water has always comforted me. By the time I made it back up to my apartment I felt like myself. I did four rounds of push-ups, pull ups, and sit-ups before hitting the shower. The warm water further relaxed my muscles. I splayed my hands on the shower wall with my head bowed to allow the water to run down my head. I mentally went through my day.

After I retired from the military, quit special ops, and finally found a therapist that I could rock with, I started my own security and investigative firm. I already had all the skills, why not put it to good use? My clientele typically included people of high notoriety, but I also took on regular clients and a few pro bono cases. I was head security for Senator Gerald Jackson. He sought out my firm after he started receiving some concerning emails and letters in the mail. Nothing had happened, but he didn't want to take any chances and thanks to us nothing had went down over the years. He'd kept this a secret from his family because he didn't want to worry them. Luckily, it'd been a while since he received anything. When he came to my firm, I was no longer working security and had settled into my role as owner and manager, but when Gerald asked me to head the team I assigned to him, I couldn't say no. Gerald had this TV *Black-father* figure vibe and I was drawn to him. Something in my spirit told me to accept his terms and so I did.

His family was coming to town to celebrate his birthday, so all hands were on deck this weekend. I scheduled the team to be there bright and early so that I, along with one of his daughters, could debrief them. His oldest, Rasheeda, would give us a run-down of all of their plans to verify that we had everyone in place. The weekend should go smoothly but we all knew that

Senator Jackson's youngest and only biological daughter was a wild card. She didn't come around as often as her sisters, but I learned that she lived a very carefree life and had a checkered past. Ms. Raven Jackson was definitely the reason for her father's gray hairs. I was going to make sure someone kept a close eye on her. Drying off, I slipped into my black suit and matching shirt. After straightening my tie, I grabbed one of my premade protein shakes, my gun, badge, and headed out.

As usual, I was the first one to arrive. I parked my truck and took one of the golf carts to check the grounds. I already knew the vulnerable areas, but it was my process to have someone to check the perimeter, not only during shifts, but before and after shifts. The Senator's home was on a nice piece of land. He definitely had family in mind when he purchased the home before he got married. There was a pool, basketball and tennis courts, a playground, and a separate in-law quarter which my team used if we were doing over night shifts. Mr. Jackson didn't make this type of money as a senator. He was a successful businessman, well respected, and came from old money. The Jackson lineage was loaded with wealthy entrepreneurs, both men and women. By the time I made my rounds and stepped through the front door, my team was already in the sitting room waiting for me. They knew we prided ourselves on being punctual, so they knew to be ready at least fifteen minutes before go time.

"Good morning. I'm glad to see that everyone is on time and ready to get this weekend started. All hands are on deck for the festivities. You all will be assigned to different areas and people depending on your shifts. No one enters this house without showing their ID. I don't care if they got through the gate. They need to be scanned in; everyone," I emphasized. "If you notice anything that seems or feels off, then let the team know immediately. No second guessing and no investigating on your own. If it's suspicious, call it in. Be professional and stay in your lane at all times. I don't care what anyone says to you, you treat them with respect. We protect at all cost. Mrs. Graham is going to go through all of the festivities that will be happening then I will have your assignments sent to your phones."

Rasheeda waltzed into the room with Mrs. Perry, their house-keeper, behind her pushing a cart full of bagels, doughnuts, and coffee. She wore a pleasant smile on her face. Rasheeda was shaped like a full-figured model and had an air of confidence about her that you could not deny. I caught a few of my men checking her out so hard that I had to clear my throat. I fixed myself a cup of coffee while she addressed my team. When I looked up, Mr. Jackson was standing in the doorway looking at his daughter with pride.

"Dad! You are not supposed to hear any of this. Liam already ruined the surprised with the need to have all of this security for some reason. Can you at least let us surprise you in other ways?"

"Rah, I'm too old for surprises."

"Dad, please."

"Fine. I just need to speak with Liam." He waved her off and waved me over. I followed him to the kitchen where the chef was already prepping for lunch and the family dinner tonight. Rayne was hovering in the kitchen making sure the food was just right. He walked over and she kissed him on the cheek before leaving.

"What's up Mr. G?" The Senator pulled me into a fatherly hug and patted my back.

"Not much. In a few hours I'll have all my girls under one roof, which will make me the happiest man."

It was obvious that he was referring to his youngest daughter. From what I knew, she didn't visit as often as Rasheeda and Rayne, even though she was his biological daughter. She was involved in some scandal about seven years ago and it created a wedge between the two of them. After everything that went down, she kept her distance. Mr. G was a good man so I couldn't understand what her issue was. She sounded like an overprivileged, spoiled brat to me.

"I'm sure your girls will be happy to celebrate their patriarch."

"Yeah. I just wish my precious Katherine was here to see this. She died when Raven was only fifteen, so she never really got to see them grow into the women they are today. Maybe Raven would have been different under her influence. We lost her when she and Rayne needed her the most."

Mr. Jackson looked off into the backyard contemplating. I stood next to him and bumped his shoulder.

"What's up old man?" The Senator chuckled. We'd grown close over the years and had become more like family. My father lived a few hours away and Mr. G filled that void for me when I couldn't make the time to see him.

"How are you Shooter?" he teased.

"Now you know I prefer not to go by that name anymore, Sir. I don't know why I shared that with you."

"I know. I'm just joshing you. But seriously, how are you?"

"I had a nightmare last night." A sigh escaped from my lips as I stuffed my hands in my pockets.

"The same one?"

"Yeah. I haven't had that dream in years. It's been reoccurring lately, so it's a little alarming. Therapy was working and I thought that I was getting better."

"Don't do that, Son. You are better and you are managing. You've done well for yourself and you've pretty much done it on your own. Are you dating?"

"Where did that come from and what does that have to do with anything?" A frown formed across my face as I regarded him.

"Liam it's not good for a man to be alone and have never loved."

"I've loved…"

"With parameters, Liam. Your guard is always up. You need someone who will push through that, who will challenge you. Someone who can add a splash of color to your life. Women have the power to nurture and heal. You deserve to have what I had with Kat. A love like that could help."

"From what you told me that seems impossible. Mrs. Kat sounded like she was the G.O.A.T when it comes to women."

"Hmm. I'm pretty sure there's a woman out there who would come close." He regarded me like he was holding onto some secret. I grunted then clapped my hands together.

"Okay, Mr. G, enough of the small talk. It's time for me to do what you're paying me to do."

"Sure, sure, but before you go, I expect you to participate in at least one of these events this weekend."

"Sir, I will..."

"As family, Liam and that is final young man. You're family."

Not one to argue with the boss, I simply nodded my head and headed up to the front of the house. Time to get to work.

CHAPTER THREE

"**M**ommy, are we there yet?" Sade whined. My eye twitched. I hated when she whined. This was the hundredth time she asked that question. I didn't want to snap at my baby, but I was down to my last nerve and she was twerking on it.

"We're just a few minutes away little girl. Chill."

I was late. My sisters were going to kill me. They'd been blowing up my phone since early in the afternoon and I ignored all of their calls, including my dad's. Let me just say that it wasn't my fault. I thought that before I left to be with family all weekend, I would get one in with the guy I was currently dating. That never happened because right when I was going to give him the best head of his life his fiancé showed up and I spent almost two hours hiding in the closet until he was finally able to get her out of the house. Let me also just say that I had no idea that he was in a relationship. By the time I high tailed it out of there I had to pick up Sade then go home and pack. When I glanced in the rearview mirror, I caught her pouting. She didn't deserve my attitude.

"I'm sorry, Honey Bun. Mommy is just tired. Are you excited to see your cousins?" I asked in an attempt to change the mood.

"Yep! We're going to have a sleep over and do our nails and

feet."

My sister's and I all had girls and they were all born a year after each other. My dad was outnumbered by the women of the family, but I think, deep down, he loved it. By five-thirty I was pulling around the driveway to the front of the house. Sade and I just needed to freshen up and we would be ready for dinner at six. The valet opened my door before going around and helping Sade out of the car. We grabbed our bags and took the steps up to the front door. I frowned when I noticed two big ass security guards. Well one was big as in tall and the other was just massive. At least the big guy smiled. I smiled back at big guy then turned my attention to tall and handsome. *Wait a minute*. The other guy remained stoned face and regarded me with disinterest. He was tall, slimmer than the other guy, but I was pretty sure there were perfectly carved muscles under the all-black suit he wore. His milk chocolate skin was flawless, and he wore his hair cut low and faded on the side. A lush extended goatee framed his chiseled face. Damn, he was the epitome of fine. He was perfection. With a sexy smirk on my face, I sashayed my way up the remainder of the steps. My face fell when they both moved to block my entry.

"Hi. Excuse us fellas." I attempted to move forward, but they remained in place.

"Ma'am, I need to see ID." The slim one held his hand out.

"Excuse you?" I scoffed.

"I'm not letting you in without proper clearance."

"EXCUSE ME?"

"You said that already. Identification please."

"I'm not understanding you talking about what you won't let me do. Who do you think I am? You think I would try to do some illegal shit with a kid on my arm?"

"Mommy no cursing." Sade nudged me in the leg with her bag.

He gazed down at my little girl and stared into her big, beautiful eyes that were just, innocent. She smiled up at him. *We got him now.*

"I've seen worse than that."

"Ugh!" I stomped my foot in aggravation.

"I know you know who I am. Daddy doesn't hire dummies. Imbeciles maybe, but not dummies." He continued to stare at me and Sade.

"Dad!" I screamed into the house. I'd never been treated this way by any of my father's staff. Who did this man think he was? Seeing my father's large frame fill the doorway made me smile and Sade bounced on her toes.

"Shooter! Are you giving my baby girl a hard time?"

"No Sir, just adhering to protocol. So, Miss if you wouldn't mind..."

"Miss? You know who I am."

"I also know that you are extremely late Miss Jackson." *Shooter's* lips turned up into a devious smile. It was so brief that if I would have just as much blinked, I would have missed it. My mouth gaped open at the audacity.

Daddy!" I stomped my foot, ready to throw a tantrum.

"Ray just cooperate, please. They have to get you and Sade a tag and it can't be done without the proper ID. You're not new to this." My dad gave me a firm, no nonsense look. I caved and handed over both of our identification. While mean ass did his thing, I took the opportunity to enjoy the body of this handsome man in front of me. Mr. Security was a work of art. The man looked like God carved him by hand. Like I said before, perfection. The scar on the side of his face that ran almost from his ear to the corner of his mouth was his only imperfection and even then, it seemed to add to his sexy. He looked dangerous.

"So, *Shooter*, what's your real name?"

"Mr. Washington, and I advise that you refrain from calling me anything else but that." He was going to be a tough cookie to break, but I was always up for a challenge.

"My bad. Do you have a first name, Mr. Washington?"

"Liam. Here are your tags. Keep them on you at all times."

"I know something that you can keep on me at all times." I purred and leaned in closer to Liam.

My dad cleared his throat to gain my attention. Gerald Jackson knew his daughter very well and he also knew my type. The last thing he needed was another scandal, so he ushered us into the house.

"Come on, you two. Dinner starts soon. Thank you, Liam."

"Yes, thank *you*, Liam." Once in the house I was able to appreciate Liam's *assets*.

"I'll be in shortly, Sir." He turned and addressed my dad. I didn't care if he caught me looking. I winked at him before my dad tugged me along.

"Where is your home training? I did not raise you to throw yourself at men young lady."

"Daddy it's the twenty-first century. Times have changed." I wrapped my arms around my dad and hugged him tight.

"Times have changed. What? Are you one of them feminist now?"

I smiled and shook my head. "What if I am? I just believe in doing what feels right and not necessarily what is lady-like."

"What am I going to do with you?" My dad kissed me on the cheek. He set his eyes on Sade and they lit up with affection.

"How's my beautiful and smart granddaughter?" My father grabbed Sade's hand and walked ahead of me as they caught up.

"Dad, she needs to change." I stood next to the stairs and waited for Sade to turn around. Like I expected she was already pouting. My sisters came jogging down the stairs and showered Sade with hugs and kisses.

"Where the heck have you been Raven?" Rayne was the first to speak.

"Hey sisters. I can explain." I hugged both of my sisters tightly. I'd missed them.

"We don't have time for that. You were supposed to be here hours ago. Go on and get dress so we can get started." Rasheeda, or Rah as we liked to call her, ordered.

Rayne leaned into me and whispered, "You can tell me later over cocktails."

"Speaking of cock..." I pulled my bottom lip in between my teeth as I grinned.

"Ooooh, you've met Liam." Rayne laughed and Rah huffed and stomped away.

"How did you know?"

"Because he's your type."

"And what exactly is my type?"

"Fine as hell! To be honest, he ain't your type, Sis. That is a grown man we're talking about."

"What is that supposed to mean?" My head whipped back like I'd been bitch slapped.

"You know what I mean. You are free, unpredictable, and un-tethered. Liam is disciplined and steady. I know that you just want him for the chase. Anyway, go get dressed before Rasheeda pops a blood vessel. I popped an edible earlier so everything is co-pasetic with me."

Rayne walked away without another word, rendering me speechless. I started to go after her to finish our conversation, but baby girl tugged at my arm. Not wanting to further delay dinner, Sade and I washed up at the double sinks. Her lips were poked out the entire time. She wanted to take a bath in the soaking tub.

"Sade don't make me put that lip back in for you. You will have plenty of time to get in that tub. We're celebrating Papa's birthday this weekend, so we need to put on our happy faces. Okay?"

"Okay. Can I wear my unicorn headband?"

"Sure."

I did a quick light beat on my face. I wanted to give myself an ethereal glow. Thankfully I didn't have to do anything with my hair. Since we were having dinner at home, I wanted to be comfortable and still cute, so I dressed in a yellow body suit and distressed skinny jeans. I threw on a slouchy off the shoulder sweater over it. We were eating outside on the screened in patio and the temperature had dropped. I slipped into silver pumps and matching hoop earrings. Sade wanted to match with mommy, so she was wearing her mustard yellow sweater dress with navy tights and sneakers. I tried to get her to wear her Mary Jane's but my mini me had her own style.

We jogged down the stairs and followed the hum of conversation and laughter outside. The patio was decorated with festive lights and candlelight. There was a special table set up just for the kids. I bent down and kissed my dad on the cheek then took my seat in between Rayne and Rasheeda. We've sat like that since we were kids. As the youngest I always wanted to sit by both of my sisters and it just stuck. My eyes roamed the space to take in the security. Daddy typically had one security on him at a time, so this was new. Liam's eyes met mine and I waved. My stomach did somersaults when he nodded in acknowledgment of me, but my dad cleared his throat to kill our moment.

"Dad what's with all the security like we're the first family or something? Is there something we need to know?"

"Nothing you need to worry about. I just need the extra manpower to keep an eye on my girls."

I wasn't convinced, especially after his eyes quickly diverted over to Liam. He was getting cornered later. My sisters and I helped Mrs. Perry set dishes of food on the adult table and spaghetti for the kids. They all whined when I put a little bit of green beans on their plates. We ate family style passing dishes of salad, various pasta dishes, and buttery garlic rolls. We washed our food down with a signature red blend from Rayne's winery. Yep, my bad ass sister owned a winery, so I was never without a good drink. She kept my beverage fridge stocked. Everyone was talking and having a great time. It put a smile on my face to see Sade with her cousins. I was happy to be back home and felt like a brat for not spending as much time with my family as I should have, specifically my dad. He was all I had at this point.

"Are you okay?" Rah nudged me.

"Yeah, just glad to be home. Where is Hakeem?"

"The hubby had to go to Seattle for a business trip. He hated that he had to miss this. Keem told me to tell you hey and stop being a stranger. We want to see both you and Sade more."

"I know it's just..." Thinking about why I didn't come around as much as I use to always made me emotional. My sister clutched my hand to steady me.

"You know we don't care about that Ray. I know I said some things, some out of anger, but most of it you needed to hear. You're my baby sister and I just want what's best for you and you... You're just hell bent on doing the wildest shit."

"Tell me about it." Rayne inserted herself in our conversation and I laughed.

"We love you no matter what you do. Understand?"

"Yeah, I hear you."

"You and Rayne are closer, so I know you two talk all the time. I want you to know that I am proud of you Raven. I may not always act like it, but I do accept who you are. Because I am your big sis, I'm always going to want you to do better. That's just me as a big sister. I'm the same way about Rayne. Sade is blessed to have you as a mom."

"No, I'm blessed to have her. She has forced me to slow down. Thank you, Rah. That means a lot coming from you."

Sade was the product of a two-year love affair with a married man and not just any married man. Tariq Wilds is a one of the most sought out and highest paid Black actors in Hollywood. He and I met on the set of a play when I was pursuing a career in acting. He took my green ass under his wing and before opening day he had me spread eagle on his bed while he turned me out. I was completely smitten with him. It would be a lie if I said that I didn't know that he was married. I did and I didn't care. Tariq was Hollywood's bad boy, and I had his attention.

He started off as a child actor, so I literally grew up watching him on TV and in movies. When it was just the two of us nothing mattered; not the fact that he presented as happily married, not the fact that he would put me up in hotel rooms for easy access while he was on his family vacations, not that he was betraying his wife, nothing mattered but us. I was a selfish bitch and didn't care.

When I discovered that I was pregnant I was so afraid to tell him, but to my surprise he was happy, ecstatic. Happiness that I misconstrued for something more because when I started rambling and planning for him to leave his wife, he pumped the breaks on my parade and us. We were over in the blink of an eye. I was heartbroken, devastated and embarrassed. Then my phone started blowing up with a link for TMZ and I shitted bricks when I read the headline: *Highland City Senator's Daughter Steamy Affair with Tariq Wilds Results in a Love Child.* Did I mention my family had no idea of this relationship or that I was pregnant?

Paparazzi had been following us for years and saw their opportunity when we were snapped walking out of my doctor's office. The picture of him kissing my stomach before helping me into the car was plastered on all social media and tabloid magazines. They even had pictures of the sonogram. I was livid and felt the need to protect my unborn child. Then there was the fall out with my dad. He was so disappointed in me. We'd had a huge fight that ended up with me feeling ganged up on by him and my sisters. I went through my pregnancy isolated, without my family. Things hadn't been the same since then.

To this day, I think it was Tariq's wife who leaked everything, but she claims she didn't, and Tariq chose to believe his wife. Tariq and I continued seeing each other off and on until Sade was about four and I grew tired of being a sideline chick who couldn't date other men. I'd finally saw Tariq for the selfish, arrogant ass that he was, and I moved on. There was still love between us, but we were now focused on coparenting Sade as best as we could. Even though the circumstances were horrible we created a beautiful masterpiece. Tariq was a great father and adored Sade, so in the end things worked out.

Goosebumps prickled the back of my neck. When I turned around, there stood Liam. He was blending in with the background to stay out the way and continue to keep a watchful eye, but I caught him staring at me. My mouth twisted when I tried to hide my smile.

"I'll be back ladies." I winked at my sisters and excused myself from the table.

Liam stood out in the yard by the flower garden dedicated to my mother. The jasmines had bloomed and paired with the gardenias created the prettiest floral scent. Purple roses, white hydrangeas, and peonies where meticulously planted. Orchids of various colors decorated the gazebo that Liam was leaning against. I kicked off my shoes and made my way over. His eyes stayed on me with every step that I took. For reasons that I could not verbalize, I was very much attracted to this man and he was, at least, curious about me. It felt like he was willing me over to him; a silent call that only I could home in on. As I reached the gazebo, I brushed past him and took a seat on the bench.

"Hi, Liam," I spoke sweetly.

"Ms. Jackson," He grumbled. When he didn't turn around to acknowledge me, I scoffed.

"Please call me Raven and I would prefer if you looked at me when you spoke."

"I see you, Raven." Liam turned around and looked me dead in the eyes. His response was simple, but it felt like the words he spoke held more meaning than what he was saying. I hummed.

"Well then come sit with me, please."

I watched as his shoulders raised then fell. He sighed. Sighed like I was being a nuisance, but I wasn't deterred from my mission.

"My dad is paying you to protect him, right?"

"Yes, Ma'am."

"And would it be safe to assume that this weekend you were hired to protect his family as well?"

"Your assessment would be correct." This time he glanced at me with interest. Maybe even amusement, but just that quick he was back to facing the opposite direction.

"You're giving me your back, Mr. Washington."

"What?" He'd finally turned around. My leg crossed over the other. I was jumping with excitement inside.

"How can you protect me when you have your back turned?"

The smile was faint, but I caught it and I just knew he had a beautiful smile. He walked towards me and stood near the bench across from me where we could face each other. It didn't go unnoticed that he chose not to sit next to me.

"This is one of my favorite spots. Whoever your father hired to construct the garden did an amazing job." When I blushed and released a shaky breath, he raised his eyebrow and tilted his head to the side.

"I did it."

"What?"

"The garden was designed and created by me. Losing my mother at fifteen was difficult for me and my therapist thought I needed a creative outlet. She noticed that I was always drawing flowers or gifting her with arrangements I would put together myself, so she suggested the idea of creating a garden in memory of my mom. I planned everything out, researched all of my mom's favorite flowers, created the sketches and blueprints then presented it to my dad. I'll never forget the look on his face when it was completed or when the flowers began to bloom."

"It's apparent that your father holds you in high regard."

"Really?"

"You don't think so?"

I shrugged. "I mean, I guess. What I'm trying to say is that I haven't been the model daughter. Made a lot of mistakes in my younger years. Wasted a lot of his money." I laughed to myself.

"I can actually talk to you when you're like this."

"Like what?"

"Not eyeing me like a piece of meat."

"I'm pretty sure it's a nice grass fed, thick, grade-A slab," I purred.

"Okay. Break over." Liam stood up and held his hand out and I gladly took it before standing up. I was disappointed when he let go, but I didn't let it show.

"I'm just kidding. I'm not as thirsty as you think I am. Am I attracted to you? Yes, and I want you to know that. Life is too short, so I live an open lifestyle. I think that you're attracted to me too, Mr. Washington."

"Ms. Jackson, it appears that your family is looking for you."

Liam placed his hand at the small of my back to usher me ahead of him. He walked me halfway then made his way over to another guard that was approaching him. I put an extra swish in my hips because I knew they were probably both watching me. Sade came running towards me and I scooped her up.

"You are growing! Eventually mommy won't be able to pick you up like this." She squealed and giggled as I spun her around before placing her on the ground.

"Is it okay if I sleep in Mya's room? We all want to be in the same room."

"As long as you promise not to stay up all night I don't mind."

"Yes! Thank you, Mommy." We walked back to the table hand in hand.

Dessert and coordinating drinks were being served. I made my way over to my dad and sat next to him with my slice of red velvet cheesecake.

"Hey, Daddy. Are you enjoying yourself?"

"This old man couldn't be happier. Thank you for coming."

"Dad, you don't have to thank me. I'm your daughter."

"A daughter who went from calling every day and visiting every other weekend to calling once a week and visiting only on major holidays. I hope to see you before Thanksgiving, Baby Girl."

"There's nothing I can say but I'm sorry. I promise to do better."

"Your old man is getting old. I don't want to waste any more time."

"Dad I don't want to think of you not being here on this earth with me." I placed my dessert on the table. Suddenly I'd lost my appetite. My dad pulled me into a hug which I returned.

"Love you more than words, Raven. You can always come home no matter what."

"Love you too, and I realize that now."

My dad helped himself to a forkful of my cheesecake.

"Liam?" His expression was that of knowing. Dad was perceptive and he knew me well.

"What? He's cute daddy."

"He's a reserved and private man, Baby Girl."

"Okay, I get it dad. I just want to see him relax a little. Speaking of relax he looks a little hungry. I'll be back."

As I walked away, I heard my dad mumble how I was never one to back down from a challenge. I perused the dessert table contemplating which dessert would be to his taste. I decided to go with the cinnamon rum chocolate cake. It was Rasheeda's prized recipe that contained a hint of vanilla. I grabbed a plate of cookies for the other guy because I really didn't care what he wanted. Walking up to the two of them I handed him the cookies and Liam the chocolate cake.

"I thought you could use a little treat. Goodnight, Liam." He looked down at the decadent slice. The corner of his lips lifted just enough to be noticeable.

"Thank you. Goodnight, Ms. Jackson."

CHAPTER FOUR

Liam

Chocolate cake was my favorite. This woman seemed to have a knack for getting inside of my head and I hadn't known her for twenty-four hours yet. She had a gift for reading people that I don't think she was aware of. I needed to keep my distance; Raven Jackson was trouble. After last night I understood that there was probably another unsaid reason as to why Gerald wanted more security. Triple R got their hands on some weed brownies courtesy of Raven and Rasheeda thought that she was dying. Any other circumstance I would have found the humor in it but not when I had to ask two of my men to stay well past the end of their shift so that Mr. G could rest without worrying about what the hell his daughters were up to.

The next morning, I arrived at the house bright and early. After securing outside, reviewing the cameras, and completing the walk-through of the inside of the house, I followed the aroma of bacon to the kitchen. My mouth opened ready to greet Mrs. Perry but I stopped when I saw that it was Raven. She was at the stove frying chicken and making waffles. Her back was towards me, but I knew who it was due to her small, but toned and shapely stature, and her bronze tapered cut or whatever color it was. There was music playing from a Bluetooth speaker that sat on the kitchen island. Dressed in running shorts and a sports bra she danced like she didn't have a care in the world. Raven swayed her hips to the sounds of afro beats hypnotizing me. The rhythm and groove seemed natural to her. As the beat picked up, she did some type of two-step and spun around while swirling her hips.

"Aaaah! Shit!" She jumped and a couple of perfectly cooked waffles fell off of the plate that she was holding.

"What the hell, Liam! You nearly gave me a heart attack." She held her hand over her chest and placed the plate on the counter.

I didn't speak. Really, I couldn't. I was still entranced by her natural, simplistic beauty. The show she'd just put on had me gathering my bearings.

"Like what you see?" She hummed.

That snapped me out of it. She was now putting the food into fancy dishes. There was a slick smirk on her face. When I didn't respond she kept talking.

"I thought I would make you guys breakfast since the family is scheduled to have brunch in the garden later. I don't recall seeing any of you eat last night. We have chicken and waffles, potatoes, eggs, and bacon. I made my famous orange pineapple carrot ginger juice. Oh! There are muffins too. You know, in case you need a snack." *You are the snack, fuck that a whole entrée.* What they hell was I thinking? My thought's alone was breaking my number one rule. I cleared my throat and my mind.

"Thank you. The team will appreciate that. *I* appreciate that. It smells great."

"You're welcome and thank you. My mom taught me how to cook. Umm, did you sleep here?"

I had slept in the guest house and was dressed in basketball shorts and a t-shirt. The next shift was starting in a couple of hours, so I had time to get a nice jog in around the lake. The morning weather was perfect, sunny but with a nice cool breeze.

"Yes, the guest house. I'm going for a run, so I'll eat afterwards."

"Mind if I join you?" I looked at her quizzically.

"Join me?"

"Yes, I'm not just wearing this outfit to be cute," she quipped. I took the opportunity to take in her appearance. Raven's physique was definitely one of someone who worked out regularly. Running was typically my private time, but she looked like she seriously wanted to tag along. I motioned my head towards the front door.

"I hope you can keep up."

Raven kept up and talked the entire time. I learned that she owned a holistic wellness center for women which was impressive. She was almost a jack of all trades having had careers in acting, the visual arts, music, and a few businesses that included an apothecary and candle business. Hearing about all of her different jobs and her wanderlust almost gave me anxiety. For lack of better words Raven was flighty. No one would label her as reliable. Definitely not my type. After we put in three miles, we went our separate ways to get our day started.

Since today was Mr. G's birthday, I agreed to join him and his family for brunch. I made me a couple of to-go plates of the meal that Raven prepared but went with a protein shake for breakfast. So far, the weekend was going well, but that only meant we needed to be more vigilant. Whenever it seemed like you could relax is when shit usually hits the fan. By the time I made it to the garden Gerald and his family were already out there enjoying each other's company. The girls ran around in their matching purple dresses chasing butterflies and the adults were gathered around each other sharing a laugh. Triple R went all out. Furniture was rented and set up to give it a lounge vibe with colorful patio furniture and loungers. It was all housed under a tent with balloons and a happy birthday banner. My eyes scanned the area, and I acknowledged my team with a nod. A loud infectious laugh caused my head to turn and there she was. Raven's eyes sparkled as she laughed with her dad and sisters. When she snorted, I fought to hold in my own laughter. She was wearing a flowing floral dress with a split up her thigh. She was barefoot and wore gold accessories from her ears down to her ankles. Raven wasn't my match but dammit if she wasn't a sight to behold.

"Beautiful ain't she?" My eyes cut to the left of me at the man who interrupted my thoughts. I had to stop myself from growling at the sounds of Allen's voice. Allen Henderson was the advisor and assistant to Gerald. They'd known each other since Allen was in college when Gerald mentored him. From my research I discovered that he sought Gerald out and that never sat well with me. I couldn't stand him. There was something about him that came off as slimy. A few months after I started working for Gerald, I sat with him and explained how I did not trust Allen and wanted to dig deeper into his background, but Gerald called me paranoid and asked that I trust his judgement. Allen was also the snake type. He slithered around in the shadows then made his presence known at the most inopportune time. I decided to do my job and ignored him.

"Let me just get ahead of this now. Raven is different and you can't handle all of *that*." The way he looked at her made my skin crawl. He wore this arrogant look on his face, and I wanted nothing more than to slit his throat.

"Allen I would be remised if I didn't let you know that I'm being paid to do a job and that job now includes those three women. As head of the team, I will stop at nothing to hunt and take down whoever come at any of them in a way that *I* deem inappropriate regardless of how Mr. Jackson feels about it."

My stance widened and I clasped my hands in front of me. Seeing Gerald with his family of women and girls made me want to protect them more.

"*Ten, nine, eight, seven...*" I counted down to myself. Allen blinked then cleared his throat before walking away from me. *Fucking prick.* He strutted over to Raven and her sisters and hugged them in a way that I thought was a tad inappropriate. Raven gave him a quick half hug and slickly avoided the kiss on the cheek. She gave him a warm smile. I couldn't really hear her but could tell she said something on the lines of not ruining her makeup.

"Special, isn't she?" Gerald chuckled when I grunted.

"She's something..."

"Raven has this radiance about her that she inherited from her mother. They have a way of drawing people into them. It's a gift and a curse though. Some love you for it while others hate you because that light outshines theirs. She's always been a happy kid. Went through a dark period when my Kat died, but she's a survivor."

I didn't know why Gerald was over here on his birthday talking to me about his daughter. My expression must have showed my confusion. Gerald began to walk closer to his family and motioned for me to follow.

"You like her. Don't deny it. There is something about my daughter that has kept your attention since she arrived no matter how brief your encounters have been. You may not even know what it is because you're so focused on her not being... your type, but I can tell that there's something there. A father knows."

He was right. There was something about Raven that had my attention. I was curious about her and found myself observing her whenever we were in the same room, but that was all that I could do. I had no space in my being for a woman like that. In addition, we more than likely had nothing in common.

"She's light where I'm darkness. There's things about me that..." Unable to finish I shook my head. "The shit that I carry is too heavy for a woman like that. Raven needs someone who's more like her, happy and not tainted by the darkness of this world."

"Like Leith?"

"Leith?" *As in my brother*? Then there he appeared, my twin brother and only best friend standing too close to Raven. He spoke into her ear and she tossed her head back and giggled, Leith's hand touched her arm, and she didn't shy away. I had no right to be bothered by their interactions; I barely knew her besides what was in the file I had on her. Before I realized it, I was two feet away from them. Her eyes lit up when they landed on me.

"Liam, I didn't know you had a twin brother. You two are like night and day." Which was true but coming from her made those words sting. Where I was the more serious one, Leith *was* the fun one. He didn't go to college and focused on his art instead. Leith was the life of the party while people steered clear of me, except for Raven, that is. He was the free spirit and very much like her.

"Hey. Where did you just go? Did you hear me?" Raven's hand touched my face and I frowned before stepping back. My eyes met my brother's and he already understood. He knew me better than anybody, sometimes better than myself. Raven snatched her hand back in dejection and cleared her throat.

"Sorry. I was just... I didn't mean to... You know what? I'll let you two hangout." When she turned to walk away, I reached out and grabbed her hand, stopping her. An undeniable spark flowed up my arm and into the pit of my stomach. Raven gasped. We both looked down at our hands and up at each other. I was the first to let go. She opened those perfectly shaped full lips to speak.

"Raven! Fellas! Time to eat!" Rayne shouted. Raven took a few steps backwards and smiled.

"Care to sit with me, Mr. Washington?"

Say no Liam. "Yes."

"Of course!"

My brother and I responded in unison. Raven playfully rolled her eyes before making her way to the buffet.

"The more the merrier." She sang.
Leith playfully shoved me, and I shoved him back as we followed along.

"Do you always have to play around?"

"Wouldn't be me if I didn't. I saw the way she looked at you. That's all you brother. I'm lowkey mad that you saw her first. You sure you can handle her?"

My eyes found Raven's once again. Her tongue tasted her bottom lip and she flashed me an enticing smile. In that moment I realized that I was being seduced all along and that I was caught in her net. I felt myself react below my waist and I shifted my stance. Heat flowed through my veins and my heart began to beat to a different tempo.

"Leith, I'm not sure about anything in this moment except

that this woman is going to drive me completely insane."

CHAPTER FIVE

Raven

Daddy's birthday brunch was a beautiful success. It was mostly a family affair with a few of his friends and former colleagues. We all presented him with special gifts that he absolutely adored. Seeing him so happy and proud made me feel good. My daddy deserved his accolades and flowers now. He didn't miss a beat filling in mom's role as best as he could. One of the many lessons I learned after losing mom and going through my own shit was to show appreciation and love to your loved ones while they are here. I was a blessed and lucky lady.

It was after eight in the evening and Sade and I had showered and changed into our pajamas. Sade sat between my legs getting her scalp oiled and massaged while she struggled through her guitar practice. She was visibly frustrated and flustered. To be honest, so was I. The sounds that she was producing made me cringe and was grating my nerves. Sade was a whiz kid and was used to naturally being good at everything, except for string instruments for some odd reason. I told her that she could choose another instrument if she wanted to, but she was determined to learn the guitar. She took in a shaky breath and I couldn't take it anymore.

"Honey take a break. Practicing while frustrated is not going to help. You can meditate with mommy then go to bed and try again tomorrow, okay?"

"But mommy..." She began to whine, and I could tell tears were forming in her eyes although her back was to me.

The light tapping on the door startled the both of us. Everyone had turned in for the night or so I thought.

"Come in." It came out more like a question than a statement. To my surprise Liam stuck his head in the room. His golden-brown eyes darkened when he noticed my appearance. I was bra-less, wearing a white tank with gray yoga shorts. Liam blinked and cleared his throat. His smile was warm and friendly as he looked down at Sade sitting on the floor pouting.

"I thought I heard someone playing the guitar."

"If you wanna call it that." Sade muttered.

Liam looked up at me. "Can I come in?"

"Uh, yeah. Sure." He ambled into the room. He was dressed down wearing sweats and a black hoodie. Our eyes remained glued to each other as he made his way over to us. His masculine energy and scent filled the spacious room. The atmosphere shifted so quickly I almost gasped. His presence took up space in the room. Liam's attention was back on Sade. He looked at her and smiled. I mean genuinely smiled. Not a smirk, but a whole ass corners turned up, light in eyes type of smile.

"Did you know that I know how to play the guitar?" Sade shyly shook her head.

"No sir."

"Can I?" Liam held his hand out. Sade handed him the guitar. Liam plucked at the strings and made some adjustments before he sat on the bed next to me. Sade spun around and remained seated on the floor. Liam began to play a melody familiar to both Sade and me. Her eyes lit up in recognition as Liam strummed Sade's *Smooth Operator*. It felt like Liam was singing to us through the guitar. He created a heavenly melody that had me entranced. When he was done Sade jumped up in excitement. She clapped and hooted like she was at a concert.

"Baby people are sleeping," I reminded her and laughed.

"Ut oh, sorry. Mr. Washington can you show me? Please." She pleaded with her hands folded together.

"Honey Bun, it's late." I warned.

"I can show her something quick to help with what she was practicing. We can sit out on the balcony." How could I say know to my baby's angelic face and Liam's fine ass?

"Okay. You have ten minutes and then it is bedtime young lady."

"Yay! Thank you." She slipped on her slippers and a robe then followed Liam out of the patio door. I decided to take advantage and do a few yoga stretches. My body felt extra tight from this morning's exercise and run. A Facetime call coming through cut my practice short. When I saw who it was from, I rolled my eyes and considered ignoring his call. Knowing that Sade hadn't spoken to him today was the only reason that I answered.

"What up baby daddy?"

"Aye let me ask you something Ray. Did you take your ass home to see your dad or to be laid up under some nigga?" *Wait what?* I pulled the phone further away and blinked. Tariq's face was all twisted up and the vein in his neck was pulsing. He was pissed. *Oh well.*

"What are you talking about? Have you been smoking?"

"I'm talking about that tall G.I Joe looking dude you are making googly eyes at in these pictures your sister posted. Are you fucking him? Has he been around my daughter?"

"If I am it doesn't have a thing to do with you. It's been over between us. He works for my dad."

"It's never over between us. What we felt... What we feel for each other does not go away like that."

"It does when you are *married* Tariq." I sighed and ran my hand through the curls on the top of my head. He was not going to pull me back. "Look do you want to tell your daughter good night or not?"

"Yeah man. This conversation ain't over Ray. Put her on the phone."

"It's over for me baby daddy. Hold on."

I got up from off the floor and pulled the French doors open. Sade was playing her cords. It was an improvement from earlier. I was astounded. I took a seat across from her and Liam and watched her play and look up to him for reassurance. It made my heart swell. Sade was usually very cautious around men she didn't know, but Liam had quickly won her over.

"Yo, Ray!" *Shit*. That quickly I'd forgotten that Tariq was on the phone. When Sade was done, she reached for the phone.

"Hey, Daddy! Did you hear me?" She stepped over Liam and went into the house. She was only six, but she knew her daddy well and knew he saw Liam sitting next to her.

"He sounded upset."

"He will be alright. Just want to be all up in my business." Liam's eyes wandered into the bedroom then back to me.

"She's okay. Her dad and I have a complicated situation but he's harmless. She has him wrapped around her little fingers. There were some pictures online that made him jealous."

"Pictures of what?"

"Us." I patted the empty space next to me and he joined me. He smelled so good; sexy and woodsy. I swiped through the pictures for him to see. The way we looked at each other, the way he looked at *me*, in some of these pictures I could see why Tariq was all up in his feelings. Tariq was married and had no right though. Liam did not say anything, but I could feel the heat emanating from him. The attraction I had toward Liam was undeniable and I wasn't one to beat around the bush. I was used to getting what I wanted. Right in this moment I wanted Liam. I turned in my seat to face him better. My head tilted as I regarded him.

"Tell me something about you, Liam."

"Like what?"

"*Anything*. I'm sure you know way more about me than you let on."

"True but it's my job to know."

"Is it also your job not to make friends? Come on. Talk to me." I crossed my legs and waited. Liam tapped his finger on his lip then shook his head.

"I'm a reformed troublemaker. Went into the military before my twenty-first birthday. Turns out, it was exactly what I needed. It changed my life, but it also saved my life. I'm from the area. I'm thirty-seven, I- I don't know what else you want from me, Ray."

"What's your favorite color?"

"Black."

"Debatable but okay. What's your zodiac sign?"

"Aquarius."

"Ah! Wow. That makes so much sense." My finger snapped and I pointed at him.

"I'm not following you."

"Your sign, it's a fixed sign. You're able to calm situations and you are set in your ways. You don't like to be controlled."

"How do you know this?"

"I read a lot." I shrugged. "I'm a..."

"Sagittarius. I know. Raven Angel Jackson, born November 25th, 1985. Graduated at the top of her class from Florida A&M University. Don't stay in one place for too long. You currently live in South Shores."

"Your little file on me told you all that?" I tilted my chin down and bit my bottom lip.

"And more." He nodded. Liam leaned forward as he studied me. What he was looking for, I don't know. I would give anything to know what went on in that head of his.

"You're great with kids, Liam. How many do you have?"

"None."

"How does your girlfriend feel about your odd work schedule?"

"No girlfriend."

"Wife?"

"Raven." He cleared his throat then grinned, revealing perfectly white teeth. Liam's smile was a whole other type of sexy; it made him even more attractive. Somebody needed to douse my horny ass with cold water.

"I see you *can* smile. You should do that more often. It's a really nice one. So, you're a single man?"

"I'm a single man Raven. No attachments other than my brother, his three kids, and my father."

"Leith as three kids?"

"Yeah, but that's his business."

He was protective of his brother, but I wasn't passing judgement. I liked that though.

"Who takes care of... your *needs*?" When I licked my lips, his eyes followed. They darkened before he blinked his desire away.

"Who takes care of yours?" He responded with a nod of his head. His tall frame relaxed in the chair. Liam sat with his legs wide open. I allowed my eyes to shamelessly wander.

"I do *and* I date on occasion."

"Same here, but why are we having this conversation, Raven? Truthfully, I shouldn't even be in your room. I'm sorry, this is unprofessional." He abruptly stood up and helped me up.

"I'm sorry, Ms. Jackson. Let me get you secured back inside for the night."

"We are two grown adults, Liam." I pleaded as he led me back into the room and took long steps towards the door. He was back to speaking to me in that detached tone.

"Liam..."

"Goodnight, Ms. Jackson. Goodnight, Sade." I rolled my eyes and turned away from him.

"Goodnight, Mr. Liam. Thank you!" My child waved bye and, just like that, he was gone. He couldn't get out of my room any quicker.

With a wiggle of my body and flailing arms I shook off the rejection. I was bothered but not deterred. Sade giggled in amusement.

"Okay, Honey Bun, let's get some beauty rest." I pulled the covers back and turned the lamp off once she was snuggled under the duvet. She met me halfway and I gave her a peck on the forehead.

"Goodnight, Mommy."

"Goodnight, Baby."

"Mom?"

"Yeah?" That alarmed me because she never called me mom. I hoped my baby wasn't growing up right before my eyes.

"I like him, Mr. Liam. He's nice." I smiled in the darkness and released a rush of air.

"Yes, he is. Mommy likes him too."

CHAPTER SIX

Liam

I couldn't get Raven off my mind. Her scent, her smile, the way she was with her family, specifically her daughter. Raven was like the sun and for once I was drawn to the light. She just wasn't what I needed. Hell, I wasn't what she needed. There was no way she would fit into my way of life. I would taint her with my baggage. This was a dangerous game I was playing by simply entertaining the thought of letting this woman in. Many had tried and failed, but I had an inkling that she wasn't going to take no for an answer. This beautiful stubborn woman.

It wasn't my intentions to rush out of her room the way I did, but she was weakening my resolve. She'd already cracked my armor and was slowly chiseling her way through. The way she spoke in such close proximity of me didn't make my departure easy. I prided myself on being so disciplined and put together although I wasn't always that way. My time in the service did that for me. I used to be wild and into doing illegal shit like selling drugs and robbing niggas. One thing about me, I never was reckless. That was Leith all day. I was always the more responsible one, more calculating, even when I was fucking up. The only thing I use to care about was making money, getting high, and screwing women whenever I wanted. After I was arrested for some drug charges my dad gave me an ultimatum. Get out and never comeback or join the service and make something out of myself. That ultimatum also got Leith right because there was no way he would have survived in the military. I joined the Marines and Leith learned from my mistakes, for the most part.

Raven was like a siren. She knew how to call out to you and pull you in. You don't know that you're in trouble until you find yourself wrapped up in her aura playing twenty-one got damn questions on the balcony of her bedroom. It was obvious that she wasn't used to being told no. Hell, I didn't want to tell her no. I wanted nothing more to give her exactly want she wanted, but I took my job seriously. I needed to keep my distance from her by any means necessary. Before hopping in the shower, I did a round of various pushups and sit-ups. I decided it was best that I slept in my own bed tonight, at home. Raven seemed to be persistent and I didn't trust her sneaky ass.

"Hi Mr. Liam! I've been practicing all morning. Can I play for you later? Please."

Sade greeted me at the door like she'd been waiting for me to make an appearance for the day. Like she had ants in her pants, she bounced on the balls of her feet. She was dressed in plaid tights, a long t-shirt and colorful sneakers. I grinned and nodded.

"I can't wait to hear what you've been working on. Remember what I told you?"

"Uh huh. I can do anything I put my mind to." I could hear Raven's voice and knew she was making her way over. Gerald was ahead of her. She was dressed similar to Sade with her tights, t-shirt, and high-top Nikes.

"Good morning, Gerald. Ms. Jackson. Gerald do you have time to meet now?" Raven's mouth dropped before she propped her hand on her hip and frowned. Her dad's eyes ping-ponged between the two of us.

"Of course. Let's go to my office."

Once we were behind closed doors, I handed him the file I was carrying. While he flipped through, I explained about the threatening emails that he was still receiving. The first one after weeks of nothing came on the day the family arrived.

"Has anyone else mentioned receiving strange emails or packages?"

"No, not at all. I've never hurt anyone. Who could possibly send something like this? Now they're mentioning Raven. I didn't want to involve her or her sisters in this."

"Yes. You've said that, but I know you want them safe. I think they should know sir. I can put men on them, but they are very sharp women. I think they would spot a security detail immediately.

"No, I'm not doing that." He vigorously shook his head. "My children have always had a normal life. I need to keep it that way. We need to protect them from this."

My jaw flexed and I rubbed my hand down my face. "You're frustrating me old man."

"I thought that was my daughter's job. Don't think I didn't see you rushing from her wing of the house last night." He looked at me knowingly and I groaned.

"Mr. G. It wasn't like that. Your granddaughter was there. I was..."

"You're a good man Liam so no explanation needed. I'm more worried about you in this situation than my daughter. Ray can be a lot to handle sometimes. You would be a huge upgrade from the men she's used to dealing with including that child's father."

"Sir."

"I know, I know. You have every intention to keep things professional."

"Yes, Sir." We both smirked. He was calling bullshit and I couldn't deny it, but I would do my best.

"Back to why we're here. This person could be dangerous..."

"Exactly why I have you here. Come on let's go. I plan to enjoy this last full day with all my girls under one roof."

I pulled my fist to my mouth and took a deep breath. The Senator was not taking this thing serious enough, but it was my job to take it serious for him. I planned to do just that.

"Liam you're going to blow a blood vessel. Relax, Son." He gripped me by the shoulder and shook me.

Even though I nodded in understanding, there was no way that I could relax. My gut wouldn't let me. I had a sick feeling that the situation was only going to get worse. There was also that nagging feeling that Gerald hadn't told me everything when I asked about potential enemies. He was leaning too much on protection, but protection was reactive in a lot of ways. I needed his honesty to get ahead of the problem. I would revisit this conversation after the weekend. Right now, I was going to do as I was asked and allow him to enjoy his family.

I led the Senator out if his office and ran into my brother. He did security on the side whenever I needed extra eyes. Despite our differences we thought alike and fed off of each other, so I was glad that he was there. He shook Mr. G's hand before he dapped me up and pulled me into an embrace.

"Yo Senator your girls know their way around the kitchen. You're a lucky old man."

"Leith." I cut my eyes at him.

Gerald was used to my brother and simply laughed. They were having a huge seafood dinner tonight before everyone went their separate ways the next day. I tensed when I saw Allen sitting in the family room. He was smiling in Sade's face, but she wasn't returning the sentiment.

"Liam calm your ass down. I'm not trying to jump on this dude while on the clock."

"I'm not going to touch him unless I have too." I unclenched my fist. Leith looked at me skeptically. He was one of the few people who knew the other side of me that remained dormant.

"Dad asked about you. He said that he hasn't seen you in about a month."

"Yeah. I'll make my way over there. He failed to tell you that we talk almost daily."

"He wants to see you, Shooter."

"Not here, Leith."

"My bad. We'll catch up later I need to finish my rounds."

"Alright."

Leith nodded towards Allen and I headed over there.

"Hey genius!" Sade's face lit up and I thought I saw Allen frown before that sinical smile was plastered back on his face.

"Liam! Are you ready?"

"Yes. Do you have your guitar?"

"Uh huh." She ran over to get it from her mom. Raven stood up and made her way over, but I halted her steps by raising my palms up.

"We'll be in the sitting room."

Sade was like a sponge. She absorbed every word and every skill that I taught her. When she made a mistake, she would start over and kept going until she was satisfied with her perform-ance. I had to make her call it quits after a couple of hours. Her cousins had spent the time outside playing and were preparing to get in the pool. When Raven came to retrieve her daughter wearing a burnt orange bikini that complemented her copper skin, I'd made the decision to busy myself somewhere else on the property. I was pretty much successful at avoiding Raven until Mr. G requested my presence at dinner.

When I stepped into the dining room the only seat available was the one next to Raven. Allen was standing over her saying something and she gave a polite smile. Her eyes were on me as I made my way over to the seat saved for me.

"Good evening everyone. Allen." My eyes told him to back his ass up. He cleared his throat and took his seat by Gerald.

"Hey Liam." Her voice was soft and sultry.

"Raven." She tiled her head and played with her napkin.

"Wow. Did I do something to offend you?"

"No Ma'am, just doing my job."

"And does your job include not speaking to me?"

"It means not fraternizing with the people I'm working for."

"Oh, that's bullshit!"

"Excuse me?"

"I think I said what I said loud and clearly. That is fucking bullshit. You have small talk with my sister, you spend time with my dad, and you've been teaching my child how to play the guitar. Then you sit at this table and don't give me the respect of looking me in the eyes when you speak until I show my ass and act up. Being professional only pertains to me? Why is that? Because you feel something for me you rather not? No one dismisses me!"

The room had grown too quiet. After a scan of the room, we both realized that all eyes were on us. Raven appeared unbothered by the audience. My jaw clenched as I tried to control my temper. I didn't like drama and I definitely didn't like being in the center of it. I leaned towards Raven and spoke close to her ear.

"I know you're spoiled and use to getting your way, but I don't take disrespect lightly. All that cursing and carrying on like a spoiled brat ain't attractive, at least not to me. Also, if you want to talk to me like an adult you can pull me aside privately, not make a scene like an insolent child."

"You don't think avoiding me all day is childish?"

"This conversation is over." I took a sip of my water and focused on anything but her.

"Liam."

Choosing to ignore Raven, I grabbed a roll from the basket and dug into the salad that had been placed in front of me. Raven sat back in her seat and spent the night shoveling her food around the plate and tossing back glasses of wine. After her fourth glass I signaled catering to cut her off, which led to her excusing herself and stomping away from the table. Her sisters looked on with amusement. What I couldn't understand was how the hell we got here. I barely knew this woman and she was already making me crazy.

Shortly after Raven's dramatic exit I excused myself to go to the pool house to review the cameras. I had several installed throughout the property and made it where the Senator could check them from his phone. Satisfied with the surveillance, I poured myself a glass of Whiskey. After downing half of the liquor, I braced my hands on the countertop. With my eyes closed I did some deep breathing to center myself and started to come down from the events of this weekend. My eyes popped open when I thought I heard movement outside. I grabbed my Glock from my holster and made my way over to the door right before it slid open.

"Shit, Raven. I could have blown your head off."

"Did you not look at the cameras?" She scoffed not fazed that she was that close to meeting her maker.

"Smart ass." I tried not to smile but couldn't help it. I stepped aside to let her in. During dinner I hadn't taken the time to really look at her. She wore a simple burgundy t-shirt dress with gold sandals and matching jewelry. She smelled earthy and sexy. Her scent took over the small space.

"Tight ass," she clipped.

"Really?"

"Yes. You need to loosen up. Might surprise yourself and have a little fun." She crossed her arms. "Why are you ignoring me?"

"Because I wasn't hired to entertain you, Raven. That's not what I do. This is unprofessional..."

"Yeah, you gave me that talk already. I don't like being ignored, especially not by you. You hurt my feelings." As she pouted she took slow steps around the room and me. I moved back into the kitchen and used the island as a barrier between us.

"Ray, it wasn't my intentions to hurt your feelings. It's just best that we keep a professional distance."

"We never finished our conversation from last night." She changed the subject.

"About?"

Raven sauntered her way around the island and stepped into my personal space. "Last night when you asked me why I initiated that conversation in the first place."

"Raven." Being this close to her, alone, was chipping away at my steely armor. My entire body reacted to her, betraying me. I widened my position to adjust.

"It's because I like you Liam and I want to get to know the real you. For some reason I'm drawn to you just like you are to me. I know you feel what I feel, even right now in this moment. You're in your head trying to explain it and find the logic in it whereas

I'm ready to explore it. There's no need for you to always be this perfect gentleman. Not with me."

If she only knew. Raven had judged me like I was some brother with the same background as her, but I can guarantee she ain't never had a man like me. She dealt with men who pretended to be bad boys because they had something to prove. As for me, I *was* about that life. I'd lived it, survived it, and it remained in me. Raven wasn't ready. I remained still while her small hands moved up my chest then up and down my arms.

"Don't you want me?" The needy look in her eyes coupled with the charged sexual energy between us made a switch in me flick on. *Fuck it.*

CHAPTER SEVEN

I saw it in his eyes the moment he threw caution to the wind. My breathing picked up and my nipples hardened with excitement. Liam's eyes homed in on them and he licked his lips.

"I will turn your ass out Raven. I'm not these little wannabe bad boys that you're used to. You're not ready for me."

Liam's thumb caressed my lips. His eyes darkened when I sucked his thick appendage into my mouth, giving him a preview of what he could have. He growled then spun me around, pulled my dress up, and ripped my panties off. I moaned my arousal. My cookie throbbed in anticipation of him slamming into me but that never came. I jumped and my body trembled when his cold tongue made a lazy trail from my swollen lips then up my back. I didn't recognize the moan that escaped from my mouth. Liam then entered me slowly and I felt every thick inch of him. He remained still until I adjusted to his size. I was beyond turned on.

"You think you can handle all this?" he whispered in my ear. He held me by the waist and eased out before pushing back into my slick folds. I whimpered as he kept this slow teasing tempo that had every nerve ending in my body tingling. Liam knew his angles. I could feel myself getting wetter with every kiss, every touch of his massive hands, every thrust... damn this man was driving me crazy. No, I couldn't handle this. No man had ever handled me this way. Before my brain could register what was happening, I screamed as my body was consumed with shocks of raw pleasure and my canal overflowed with my essence.

"Liam!" I screamed out.

"That's right. Let go, Baby." He spoke soothingly into my ear.

Liam cursed but kept his rhythm, causing another earth-shattering orgasm before his pace sped up. I threw my ass back at him and wound it in a circle. He held me tight as he released inside of me, coating my walls. I knew I messed up but, in this moment, I would gladly carry all of this man's babies. He eased out of me and backed into the fridge.

"Shit, Ray, I'm sorry. I don't know what came over me." He avoided my eyes. My face got hot.

"Excuse me? You're sorry? You could at least give me time to come down before you start regretting shit." I snatched my dress back down. It didn't go unnoticed that I just let this man have his way with me and we hadn't even kissed. I would have to be okay if this was only sex for him. That usually wouldn't be a problem for me, but Liam was different; a mystery that I was eager to break down, solve, and claim. A firm hand wrapped around my arm and forced me to look up.

"Ray, slow your ass down. That's not what I meant. It was careless of me not to use protection. You're already making me do shit I don't normally do."

"Why are you so concerned with stepping outside of your norm? Live a little, Liam. We can get tested." He laughed deviously.

"I lived a lot, Raven. My stories would make your pretty little head spin." Liam shook his head before stepping out of his jeans completely. He only had to pull them halfway down to give me what I'd been craving since I laid eyes on him for the first time.

"Really? Tell me."

"Naw, I don't wanna scare you away." He slipped and spoke in what I could tell was his normal vernacular. In my naiveté, I'd misjudged him. I simply smiled. Next, he pulled his shirt from over his head. His chest was decorated with tattoos that look more like art. I'd noticed those that were tatted on his arms, but I never expected this. I eagerly approached him and let my hands trace his tattoos. Up close and personal I could tell that many of them covered scars. He tensed when I traced the scar that went across his chest and then the one on his face.

"Just beautiful. Oversees?"

"Some, most from street life." That was all he offered, and I didn't push. Liam surprised me when he splayed his hands on the side of my face and attacked my lips with his. My mouth opened to receive his tongue and he pulled out another moan that I didn't recognize. It was needy and guttural. We kissed, nipped, and licked while our hands explored the other's body, gripping at whatever we could get our hands on. Liam lifted me around his waist and walked us into the bedroom. He proceeded to have his way with me, claiming my body, and, somewhere deep down, a piece of my soul. He was right, I wasn't ready.

Feeling like I was on cloud nine, I took my time closing the front door and tiptoeing my way up the stairs. The last thing I wanted to do was wake up my dad and have to tell him what I'd been up to. A smile graced my face when I thought about all the nasty shit Liam did to me.

"And where are you coming from sneaking back in the house at almost three a.m.?" I must have looked like a deer in headlights getting caught doing what most called the walk of shame. But I was walking the hallway like it was my runway. Rayne did scare the shit out of me though. I stared up at her and giggled. She was looking over the railing of the loft that was turned into a cozy reading nook. I climbed up the ladder-like stairs and joined her.

"Thanks for putting my baby to bed. What are you doing up?"

"Girl whatever. Sade is our baby, too. Anyway, I asked a question first. Now where did you sneak off to?"

I grinned so hard I thought my face was going to seize up. Her eyes lit up in understanding.

"Liam," I whispered.

"Bitch I need details! You finally wore that man down, didn't you? Damn, you work fast." Rayne quietly clapped her hands. We both snickered.

"Yes, and he wore me out in return. I think I'm in love, Raynnie." I fell back and the oversized cushy bean bag chair caught me.

"Ray..." My sister dragged my name out. Her toned carried a warning.

"What?" I jumped up from where I was sitting.

"You're not in love with him. You may be dickmatized. I will give you that. What has he done or said for you to be in love?"

"Love is not about what someone has done for you. It's about a connection and the multitude of feelings that comes along with it. The day I found out that I was pregnant with Sade I loved her. I didn't have to wait until her first kick or her birth for that to happen. Why can't it be the same thing with dating?"

"I'm not saying that it's not possible, but he ain't the first for you."

"You're absolutely right but this is different." When Rayne said my same words in unison, I sucked my teeth. I plopped down on the papasan lounge chair and narrowed my eyes at her. My face fell and I focused on picking at the fibers on the cushion.

"I'm serious Raynnie. I know what I feel. There's something special about Liam. It's different. I really like him." Her eyebrows hiked then she leaned in and studied my face. Her shoulders fell.

"Shit, Ray. You *are* serious."

"The sex was bomb too so there's that." We looked at each other then broke out in a fit of laughter. I snorted then clamped my hands over my face.

"Shh! What are you two up here cackling about?"

Rasheeda entered the loft and sat on the floor. Like always I was in between the two.

"Ray fucked Liam."

"Raynnie!" Rayne shrugged like she did nothing wrong by blurting out my business to our oldest sister who sometimes acted like our mother.

"Ray don't play with the man. I hope you used a condom." I bit my bottom lip then rubbed the side of my neck.

"Raven!"

"I cannot believe you. Have I not taught you anything?"

"At least you're on birth control."

"No, I'm not. It makes me fat." The corners of my mouth turned down and I shook my head. Both of my sisters stared at me with blank faces.

"I will go to the pharmacy later and take care of it. Damn."

"Let me go back to bed before I hurt this girl. I suggest the two of you do the same or you'll be waking up with bags under those eyes."

"I'm not a girl, Rah. I'm a grown ass woman."

"Well, act like it."

"Ooo, she told you."

"Y'all ain't right." I stood up and stretched my short limbs.

We all went our separate ways. Sade was in our bed sound asleep. She must have grown tired of her cousins. I watched her peacefully sleep without a care in the world. I prayed over my little angel. After a quick shower and a few yoga poses I climbed in the bed. I was asleep as soon as my head hit the pillow.

The next morning everyone was packed up and ready to go. Maybe not necessarily ready to go but ready to get back to our normal routines. I was considering staying for a few more days. It wouldn't be an inconvenience since Sade was ahead in her studies and I could have one of the managers to cover for me at the center. I'd missed my dad and felt guilty that I didn't come around like I use to, but I'd planned to change that. We all had breakfast together and were lounging around the pool. I went into the house and found my dad in his office. His eyes lit up when I stuck my head in.

"What's up, Daddy?"

"Hey, Baby Girl. Come in." I took a seat in front of him and propped my elbows up on his massive desk. I used to sit in the exact same chair as a little girl and watched him work until my mom made me go outside to play. While he worked, I fiddled with whatever I could get my hands on. Periodically his eyes would leave the monitor and land on me. Finally, he sat back, removed his reading glasses, and folded his hands over his stomach.

"What's on your mind?"

"I'm going to do better, Daddy. If it's okay I want to stay a few more days, then come back in a couple of weeks. I want to spend some quality time with you. I've missed you and I miss home."

"I've missed you too and I would love it if you and Sade stayed a little longer. Spending this weekend with everyone has me considering retiring soon. Family is everything and it's important that I spend as much time with you all as possible."

"That would be awesome. I think you should seriously consider it. You've worked hard all of your life. It is time to rest and fully enjoy the fruits of your labor. You could even drive over to South Shores to stay with us on the beach." I reached out and squeezed his hand. He patted mine in response.

The faint sound of broken glass caused me to look out the window behind my dad. A dark figure stood a few feet away and I narrowed my eyes.

"Raven," my dad croaked. He was clutching his chest and a pool of blood slowly drenched his shirt as I looked on in horror. I shot up and ran to my father's side, then pulled him down to the floor when gunfire erupted. The sounds were so loud and jarring that I didn't know if they were coming from inside or outside. I shrieked and said a prayer for my daughter and family. I laid on top of my dad until the last shot was fired. My t-shirt was covered in his blood and I was blinded by my tears.

"Dad! Daddy. No, please. Dad, look at me." I did my best to add pressure to his wound as he stared up at me. My entire body trembled.

"Ray."

"No, please don't talk." He didn't look good at all. My stomach clenched in pain.

"I love you. I love all of you, but you are my biggest accomplishment." He coughed up blood and I felt like I was going to be sick. This couldn't be happening. I needed more time. I screamed and shouted for someone to help me, but it felt like we were alone.

"Dad please don't leave me. I need you. Noooooo…" I rested my head on his stomach and held on tight as I cried. His heart was beating but not at a normal rhythm. I felt his hand rest on my head, and I sobbed hysterically.

"Gerald! Raven. Raven, baby, get up."

"No! No!"

"Let me help him, Raven." Liam fought to remove me, but I wouldn't budge. His hands cupped my face and he forced me to look at him. His eyes were wild and dark, and he was covered in blood.

"I need you to let me help him." I scooted out of the way but not too far as Liam crouched over my father. He ripped his shirt open and cursed. I covered my mouth at the sight of blood gushing out of my father's chest. There was so much blood. Liam started to work on my dad, but my dad held on to his wrist and shook his head. This couldn't be happening. Dad fought to keep his eyes open. He signaled for Liam to come closer. Liam leaned over my dad and gave him his ear. I couldn't hear or make out what he was saying. After that his breathing became erratic before he took what I knew was his last breath.

"Liam help him! Please! You said you would help him! Don't let my daddy die! Pleeease…" I punched, kicked, and screamed at him and he let me until I exhausted myself. Finally, he turned around and wrapped his strong arms around me. I cried until my throat hurt and my eyes burned. Liam helped me up from the floor and walked me out of the room. He shielded me in a way that I could not look back at my daddy's lifeless body.

"Sade. Where is she?" I tried to push off of him, but he held me tighter.

"It's okay, Ray. I got her. She's safe."

We were in front of the pool house where Sade, my sisters, and their children were safely waiting. It was obvious that the girls had been crying. Liam blocked me from the girls and sent them to the bedroom after reassuring Sade that I was okay. My sister's gasped and hollered at the amount of blood that we were both covered in. I felt so numb and empty. I could tell Liam was speaking but everything sounded so muffled. The sound of cries broke through and I released a wail that shook me to my core. My sisters pulled me into an embrace. I don't remember anything else after that. Everything went dark.

CHAPTER EIGHT

Liam

We needed to regroup and get Gerald's family to safety. There had obviously been a breach, so I only took a small group of my team with me until I got to the bottom of it. I needed to get them somewhere remote and safe and I knew just a place. I called up an old friend and told her I was on the way. She understood the life and didn't ask questions when I was short with her. We all piled up in two sprinter vans and headed towards Palm Lake. Palm Lake was a secluded area littered with a few cabins and lake houses. The area was off the grid and the perfect place to live if you didn't want to be found. Inside the vehicle the vibe was solemn. Mr. G was gone. I'd failed at my job. I looked in the review mirror to see Raven still knocked out. She went into full blown panic back at the house and we had to sedate her. I was afraid of how this was going to affect her.

Once we made it to the lake house Angie greeted us from her front yard. Angie was a part of my special ops team and a good friend. She was one of the few people that I could trust other than my family. My team and I assisted the ladies out of the van and ushered them inside. Angie pulled me into a hug and Raven's sisters cut their eyes at me.

"Angie this is Rasheeda and Rayne. Ladies this is Angie. She is a good friend of mine. Raven is still in the sprinter. I'll bring her in. Angie can you get everyone settled in and into rooms?"

"Hello and welcome. Everyone can follow me."

Making my way back to the van to scoop up Raven I came face to face with Sade and her tear-stained cheeks. My heart broke at the sight of her resting her head on her mother's lap. She sat up when she saw me.

"Where's my papa? Did those bad men hurt him?"

"They did and I'm so sorry." Her bottom lip trembled, and she leaped into my arms and cried. It might not have been my place to tell her, but I knew Raven couldn't handle telling her daughter that she would never see her grandpa again. I picked her up and handed her over to Rah before I went back and got Raven. Once everyone was secured, I met with my team on the back porch while Angie worked on lunch. As I addressed the team, I paid close attention to body language and I was glad to have my brother there to assist.

"Hey Liam, what about his body?"

"I have some connections and had him taken to the morgue as a John Doe. Even with that we had the staff to all sign NDA's just in case. We need to figure out what the hell happened and quickly. They can't bury their father until we know if he was the only target or..."

"Are you out of your damn mind? What the hell do you mean we can't bury my father?" All heads turned to Raven. She pushed off of the door frame and approached us. Her tired eyes flashed with fury.

"Raven it's the best decision right now. Everyone's safety is a priority right now." When I reached out to touch her, she slapped my hand away.

"So, my father is supposed to lay on some cold slab until *you* figure shit out?" Her accusatory tone took me aback.

"Miss, I know you ain't hard of hearing so you must be du-..." The look I tossed at Rick made him swallow his words.

"What was that? Who the fuck are you anyway?" Raven moved to approach Rick and I stepped in front of her.

"Hey, give me a minute."

If looks could kill Rick would have dropped dead. I think she even let off a growl. I gently tugged Raven by the arm. "Look at me, Ray. Hey, not him, me. Look at me." Once she focused her golden eyes on me her body relaxed a little. "It's going to be okay. Let me handle this."

Raven nodded and gave Rick her middle finger before she went back inside the house. As soon as she was out of ear shot, I was on Rick in seconds. I jacked him up and backed him against the wall.

"Let that be the last time you disrespect her or anyone in that house."

"Yo Shooter, I didn't mean..."

"Nah ain't no, 'Yo Shooter.' Just nod your fuckin' head that you understand me. Don't cross me Rick. I will cut your fingers off and make you eat them. Are we clear?"

"Yes. My bad. We cool?"

"We ain't cool my dude. Your job is done for now. I'm relieving you." Rick's brows furrowed and his mouth formed into a snarl, but he knew better than to say anything else. His response to Raven rubbed me the wrong way and had me thinking murderous thoughts. It was easy to consider murder once you've done it. Especially when your last kill was less than a couple of hours ago. We took down four men who'd breached the property and that was on me. They were the extra crew that I'd hired. I'd done thorough background checks on them so that only means that someone got to them after they were hired. I killed two with my bare hands. Thanks to the military I was an expert marksman, but I preferred hand to hand combat. It was important that I come down off of the high of those two kills or it would just get easier to put someone else down. Once you became a killer you could always justify the next kill. I took a quick walk to clear my head and decompress.

When I walked back in the house and into the kitchen all eyes were on me and for the first time, I was nervous. Raven's eyes were red and puffy, and her sisters were shooting daggers at me with their eyes. Ray wiped her nose with a tissue.

"What is Raven talking about Liam? We can't bury our father.

Are you telling us that we can't lay his body to rest? Is that what you're telling us?" Rah questioned. She held Raven protectively.

"Yes, at least not right now." My shoulders fell and I exhaled. Gerald meant a great deal to me. I'd grown to see him as a father figure, so it wasn't easy disappointing his family. I swallowed the lump in my throat and cleared my throat.

"Liam we can't… I cannot just leave him without laying him to rest. Not *my* daddy! He deserves more than that. He didn't deserve to be gunned down in his home and left alone on some fuckin' cold slab in the morgue!" Raven swayed from where she stood, and I rushed to catch her before her legs gave out on her. Her sisters shrieked and released a collective gasp. I scooped her up in my arms.

"I got her. She's just exhausted. I'm going to lay her down." Rasheeda stepped forward prepared to say something but I issued a warning with my eyes and Rayne stopped her. When I found the room set aside for her, I placed her in the center of the bed. Her eyes fluttered open right as I was making my exit.

"Can you stay with me?"

"Raven. I…" I shook my head and remained planted by the door.

"Please? I know you have things to do, but I don't want to be alone. Looking into her sad yet hopeful eyes there was no way I could deny her. If I was honest with myself, I didn't want to. In the room with her was where I wanted to be right at this moment.

"Alright, I'll stay. Let me do a walk-through and put Leith in charge."

"Okay, but hurry. Don't keep me waiting."

"Sounding more like yourself already." I winked at Raven and rushed out of the room. My team and I met and secured the premises. I reminded them that our location was not to be shared by anyone. They also had to turn in their phones and received burner phones. Leith hung around after everyone dispersed. Angie had smaller cabins on her property were the team would be staying with the exception of myself and Leith. We were staying in the main house.

"I'll be the lookout for tonight. You straight though? I know you and Mr. G was close."

"I'm not going to lie bro'; it's fucking with me. I'm struggling with this shit. I can't believe he's gone."

"This is some fucked up shit. It's crazy how they went from having this epic family weekend to losing their patriarch the way they did. Raven witness that shit?"

"Yeah, and I haven't had the heart to ask her exactly what happened. I just drew my own conclusion from the scene."

"What are you thinking, Twin?"

"It's an inside job, someone Mr. G knew." Leith nodded.

"Want me to get in contact with Glitch and have him to do a deeper dive on everyone?"

"Yeah. Hit him up in the morning. If you need me, I'm with Ray."

"Aight man. Y'all be easy."

Raven's room door was closed so I knocked. A shaky voice urged me to enter. Raven was curled up on the window seat with tears running down her cheeks. I was worried about her mentally. She'd just experience a traumatic event that led to the death of her father. She looked so small and broken. I was glad that her sisters were there to help with Sade. Although they loved the Senator, they still had a living father. Raven had lost both of her parents. I filled in the space next to her and pulled her onto my lap. She melted into my embrace and cried herself to sleep. I took her to bed and crawled in behind her, pulling her close. It wasn't until I heard her light snores that I allowed my body to succumb to sleep.

A light tap on the door jolted me from my sleep. The sun was starting to set. My stomach growled. I hadn't eaten in hours.

"Come in," I grated. Angie stuck her head in.

"Hey. Is she okay?" I shook my head.

"You two need to eat. You missed lunch. I brought you dinner." She stepped into the room carrying a tray with bowls of soup, fresh bread, and two bottles of water. I took the tray from her hands and sat it on the nightstand.

"Thanks." Angie leaned on the wall and propped her hand under her chin.

"What have you gotten yourself into, Liam?"

"Not right now, Slay."

"Oh, so we using aliases now, *Shooter*."

We stared at each other until we both smile and hugged. I rocked her in my arms and kissed the top of her head.

"Damn it's been too long since you paid me a visit."

"I know, but you know I have my shit." There was movement from the bed. I turned as Raven sat up. She looked back and forth between Angie and me.

"Sleeping beauty has awakened. Hi, I'm Angie, Shooter's friend."

"Shooter? She can call you that?" Ray turned her attention to me. For some reason she was looking for a fight, but she wouldn't be getting her way.

"Sorry, I meant Liam." Raven nodded. She stared at me before she spoke again.

"Thank you for letting me and my family crash here. I hope we didn't inconvenience you."

"Nope, not at all. I'd do anything for this guy right here." Raven's eyes met mine again.

"Well, thank you." Just like that Angie was dismissed by Raven. I could feel the territorial energy surrounding her. I mouthed an apology to Angie as she made her way out.

"That wasn't necessary."

"I just don't want any extra company right now unless it's my baby. Where is Sade?"

"Rasheeda and Rayne have her."

"I know she'll want to sleep with me tonight. I'm sure she's worried."

"She is, but kids are resilient. I hope I didn't cross the line, but I explained what happened."

"Thank you because I don't think that I would have been able to." Raven wrapped herself in a hug and rubbed her arms as if she was cold. She took in the room, then shook her head in what looked like disbelief.

"Hungry?"

I held up a bowl filled with tender shredded chicken, carrots, potatoes, and spinach. Raven licked her lips then nodded. I handed her the bowl and picked up the other. We ate in silence. Just the sound of chewing and the spoon tapping the bowl. Raven placed her unfinished bowl on the nightstand.

"Ray, baby you have to eat."

"I've lost my appetite. I just want to shower, get Sade ready for bed, and cuddle with her."

"Of course. I'll go get her. I think Angie mentioned them watching movies. I know she needs to be close to you."

"And I need her, too."

She handed me her bowl and I grabbed the tray and walked towards the door.

"Liam."

"What's up?"

"Thank you for everything. The way I spoke to you earlier was wrong. We don't place any blame for what happened today on you. I need you to understand that."

"I hear you. Get all the rest you need."

CHAPTER NINE

"Grandpa! Grandpa! Please don't leave me!"

I jumped out of bed in attack mode. It took a few seconds for me to acclimate and realize where I was. Sade was on her side of the bed tossing and turning. Her face looked pained. I crawled over to her side and gently shook her until she awoke.

"It's okay, Honey Bun. It was all just a bad dream."

"Not it's not! He's still gone. Mommy I want my Papa." She bawled in my arms. I stroked her hair to soothe her. More than anything, I wanted to absorb her pain. The door opened and my sisters joined us on the bed.

"Good morning." Rasheeda placed her arm around my shoulders.

"Good morning. She'll be okay guys."

"What about you?" Rayne inquired.

I couldn't answer without breaking down again, so I simply shook my head. Both of my parents were dead, and I never felt more alone. I had no idea that I would find myself an orphan at thirty-five. The feeling was indescribable.

"Whatever you are thinking, stop. You have us. We are still your sisters and our dad loves you like his own. I know you're grieving but don't forget that, Ray. You still have a family." Rah squeezed my hand and started to pray.

More tears fell and Rayne wiped them away.

"I love you," I sniffled.

"We love you too."

We sat that way until the sun began to peak through the white curtains. My two nieces eventually woke up and joined us. In that moment, I never felt more grateful for them, for this amazing feminine energy that I never knew I needed.

There was another knock on my door and before I could respond, Liam walked in holding two cups of coffee, wearing nothing but cotton pajama pants. He stopped in his tracks, spilling a little of the coffee. He placed one mug on the dresser and licked his hand. I'm pretty sure we were all drooling at this point. Liam's eyes met ours as he caught our reaction. He blushed then blessed us with that perfect smile. My, my my, how he quickly shifted the energy in the room.

"Oh, my lord," Rah muttered in my ear.

"My apologies ladies. I'll just… I'll come back. Good morning." Just as quickly as he entered, he was gone. Rayne sat up in the bed and faced me.

"Girl! You slept with all that?" She moved her hands over her chest and stomach. "And that?" She swirled her hands around her pelvic area. "Got damn that man is fine! You are my shero."

"Girl hush! Don't you have a fiancé?"

"He ain't here and I still have eyes to see."

"Is that normal? To be so…"

"Blessed?" I interrupted. We all looked at each other before we busted out laughing and woke up the kids. It felt good to experience some happiness in the mist of tragedy.

After we got the kids washed up and dressed, I headed to the kitchen. I felt bad about giving Angie the cold shoulder when she had opened up her home for us. Seeing her so close to Liam and knowing that she knew things about him that I wasn't privy to, caused the green-eyed monster to rear its ugly head. I was jealous.

It was obvious by the aroma that Angie had already started

cooking. She was placing what looked like biscuits in the oven when I entered.

"Morning. Do you need some help?"

"Hey! Good morning. Nope. I got this. You sit down and relax."

"Let me restate that. How can I help? Look, I need to stay busy. I'm a great cook, just tell me what you want me to make."

Any idle time was going to result in me falling deep into the abyss of my sadness and grief. I needed to stay busy and I was not taking no for an answer.

"Okay you can work on the steak, but please let Liam know that you asked to help. That man doesn't want you to lift a finger."

"Yeah, right. I find that hard to believe," I scoffed.

Everything was already set out for me, so I warmed up the grill pan, seasoned the meat and went to work. Cooking allowed me to take my mind off of grieving and focus on something else, even if it was just temporarily. The steak sizzled in the pan and I inhaled its deliciousness. Angie came on the side of me and started preparing grits. She looked at me and smiled.

"So, you and Liam?"

"No? Yes. I don't know. It's weird to say this but at this point it's complicated. I'd just broken through his armor, then all of this went down."

"I'm so sorry about your dad."

A knot formed in my throat and my heart pounded to an irregular beat. My eyes blinked away the tears that threatened. I didn't know how to respond so I nodded my head and focused on the task at hand. Angie continued with the conversation.

"Yeah, it takes a long time to break through Liam's steely armor. It took me at least a year for him to consider me a friend. How long have you known him?"

"Um, just a few days." I cleared my throat. I placed the finished steaks on a plate and started cutting up some fruit.

"Excuse me? Did you say a few days? Wow. That's just... wow." Angie turned and looked at me like she was noticing me for the first time. Then she shared how they met, and I told her a little about myself. She seemed cool and overall, I liked her energy. Just not the energy whenever Liam was around. There were obviously some feelings there. Everyone began to fill into the kitchen and family room. When the time came to eat, I no longer had an appetite, so I filled my plate with fresh fruit. All I could think about was the last meal we all had together and what I would have done differently if I knew it would be the last I had with my father. My chest felt tight and there was now a hole in my heart, a missing piece.

I smelled him and felt his presence before he entered the room. Just as he walked in, I glanced up. He was making his way towards me before Angie blocked my view. She walked him to the counter to fix him a plate. I couldn't hide the disdain on my face if I tried. I stabbed a piece of pineapple and shoved it into my mouth. When Liam sat next to me and not her, I could not help the look of victory on my face. He inhaled the majority of his food in about four bites before he looked at my plate and looked at me.

"Tell me you ate more than that."

"No. Just the fruit," I quipped.

"Raven you barely ate yesterday. You need to eat."

"I'm not hungry, Liam." He was starting to get on my nerves acting like he was my caretaker. All I wanted to do was enjoy his company.

"You should try to eat something. I'll fix you a plate."

"I said I'm not fucking hungry! Shit!" Once again, I was the cause of the room falling silent. Liam looked at me with lethal eyes.

"Ray," Rasheeda chastened.

"I'm sorry. I *can't* eat. I literally can't eat. I need some damn air." Pushing away from the table, I rushed out of the back door and didn't stop until I was near the edge of the lake. It was then that I released a blood curdling scream that echoed in the open space. My cry became caught in my throat leaving me unable to breath out. I heaved; my chest tightened. Liam caught me from behind and sat me on the ground. "They took him away from me. It hurts so bad Liam." I rested against his chest and bawled until I was out of breath and drained, but I also didn't feel as weighed down. Liam kissed the side of my face and began to hum a melody, possibly a Sam Cooke song. He actually sounded good. Between the sound of his voice, his steady breathing, and the lake, I was feeling better. Liam's lips pressed into the side of my neck and he rocked me in his arms.

"How are you feeling?"

"Honestly, I don't know. This all feels like a bad dream."

"Ray! Tariq is on the phone." Liam and I both turned around and Rayne was approaching us with my phone in her hand. Liam's body tensed behind me. My face fell in my hands.

"Ah shit. He was supposed to pick up Sade today. I never called him." With Liam's help, I stood up and took the phone. I ignored Liam's glare.

"Tariq, I..."

"Yo what the fuck is going on? Is what they're saying about your dad true?"

"What? What are they saying?"

"That he was attacked, and his family is being secluded for safety. Where is my fucking daughter, Raven?"

"Don't fix your mouth to talk to me like that, Tariq. Sade is safe with me. Tariq my dad was killed." There was a brief pause before he spoke.

"Damn. Yo Ray, I'm sorry. I didn't know, but I think my daughter should be with me." As much as I wanted to argue with him for wanting to separate my child from me at a time like this, I knew it was for the best.

"Ray?"

"Okay, you can take her." I looked up at Liam who shook his head. "We can meet up and exchange her." Liam nodded his head in approval. "I'll text you the address."

"Just give it to me now."

"No. No one can know our location and you cannot tell anyone about my dad. Not even Melanie."

"That's my wife."

"And you've kept worst secrets than that from her. Don't tell her shit."

"Whatever, Ray. I want her today."

"Fine, but not today. I will text you the address in a few."

"Thank you, Ray. And Ray?"

"Yes, Riq."

"I love you and I'm here if you need me."

"I know. I love you too. I'll see you later." Once I hung up, my phone was snatched from me.

"What the hell!"

"What the hell are you still doing with this? I instructed everyone to turn in their phones."

"I needed it just in case her dad called. Don't snatch shit from me, Liam."

"I need you to be smart about this. Your phone can be tracked. How could you be so…"

"So what?" I titled my head to the side. My body language dared him to come out of pocket. Liam pinched the bridge of his nose.

"Careless, Raven. I was going to say careless."

"I'm sorry, okay?"

"Stop being sorry and start making better decisions." Liam brushed past me and stalked back towards the house.

"Ugh! Who the hell does he think he is?"

"A man who cares about you. He's right, Raven. That was stupid."

Instead of responding, I picked up a rock and chucked it into the lake. Rayne looked on in amusement.

"Come on. It's beautiful out here. Let's take a walk lil' sis."

After our walk I went to find my daughter. She had a way of making me feel whole and grounded. A smile formed on my face when I found her on the porch playing her guitar. With Liam's help she now had the confidence she needed to progress, and she was soaring. My baby was definitely a genius in every right. She stopped when she saw me.

"Sade that was beautiful."

"Thank you, Mommy. Mr. Liam taught me."

"Mommy thinks Liam is a great teacher." I sat beside her on the porch swing and draped my arm around her shoulders. She rested her head on my side.

"I talked to your dad today and he wants you to come and stay with him for a little bit. He'll enroll you in virtual school until you come back home. How does that sound?" She shrugged then spoke softly.

"Hmm it sounds good. I miss Daddy, but I don't want to leave you."

"Are you worried about me?"

"Yes, Ma'am."

"Mommy is going to be fine. I have your aunties and Mr. Liam to look out for me."

"Mr. Liam likes you." She sat up and flashed her toothless grin.

"And how would you know that little lady?"

"Because he looks at you like this." Sade looked at me then batted her eyelashes rapidly. She looked at me like I look at cake. I tossed my head back and laughed until I snorted.

"He does, Mommy. For real."

"Okay smarty pants. Come on. Take a break and let's see what everyone is up to."

We ran into Liam on the way in. Sade hugged his legs then ran to find her cousins.

"Hey, I was coming to look for you."

"You found me. What's up? You want to apologize for being mean."

"Nah. You messed up. Your sisters and I were talking. I have an idea."

Dressed in white, we all made our way down to the lake carrying floating lanterns and torches. Liam's team lit the torches around us. It was Liam's idea that we all gather to pay our respects to my father. Rasheeda opened things up with a prayer that left everyone either sniffling or wiping their eyes. Liam stayed by my side along with Sade. We all took turns saying something about my dad.

"Daddy, I'm going to miss you. I'm sorry that I wasn't always the daughter you raised me to be, but you don't have to worry about that anymore. I just wish we had more time. What makes me smile is knowing that you're with Mom now, so tell her I love her, and I miss her. You both have left a legacy that includes strong Black women, and we are going to raise our daughters and sons to be even more amazing. We will always live by the morals and values you instilled in us. I will honor you in everything I do. You can rest now, Daddy. I love you."

We wrote messages, wishes, and prayers on pieces of paper and placed them in the lanterns. After they were lit, we released them into the lake. My sisters and I held hands as we watched the lanterns drift downstream, as we hummed one of his favorite songs. We then gathered around the firepit and just hung around sharing funny stories about Daddy. Most were about how I drove him and Mom crazy. I looked around and noticed that Liam was nowhere to be found, so I got up to see what he was up to. I found him in the kitchen. His hands braced the counter and his head hung low. I was about to say something slick when I heard him take in a shaky breath and his shoulders shook. It felt wrong to intrude so I slowly backed away and tried to exit quietly but my energetic child came running in like a bat out of hell.

"Mr. Liam! I was looking for you." Liam stood up straight and cleared his throat. He kept his back to us. I stopped her from approaching him and stooped down.

"Um, Sweet Pea, let's give Mr. Liam a minute. He can meet us outside when he's finished in here. We'll wait for him."

"Oh. Okay." I could tell that she picked up his mood. "I'm going to make him a smore," she whispered to me before running back out. I turned to follow her, but I couldn't leave. My feet propelled me back towards Liam and I wrapped my arms around him and rested my face on his solid back. I inhaled his scent and smiled. He tensed in my embrace, but I refused to let go.

"He loved you, Liam, and he'll always be with you." I gave him a gentle squeeze before releasing him and then rubbed his back. I was hesitant to leave him, so I grabbed a seat and sat there quietly. He eventually turned around and approached me. His hand caressed my face as he gazed into my eyes. He kissed me on my forehead and squeezed my thigh.

"You think Sade has that smore waiting for me?" I smiled and nodded. With my fingers interlaced with his I led him outside.

"Oh, definitely. She's probably focused on making you the best one. Come on."

CHAPTER TEN

Liam

Raven and Sade sung along to the radio. We sat in the car in the outlet mall parking lot waiting for Sade's dad to show up. She was a ball of excitement. While she ate her ice cream she bounced around in the backseat. This setup felt a little too comfortable for me, but these two had a way of drawing you in. The deepest part of my core needed to be close to them, to their energy.

"She seems excited." I nodded my head towards the backseat. Raven smiled and nodded her head.

"She loves her dad. Makes me jealous sometimes."

"I'm pretty sure that there's no comparing the two of you." Raven blushed and swayed to the music. A black Bentley pulled up across from us.

"That's Tariq. Come one Honey Bun, your dad's here."

"Yay!"

"Wait." I held my arm out to stop her. "How can you be so sure?"

"Because only my baby daddy would be in a small lake town being chauffeured around in a Rolls-Royce Ghost."

When I pulled out my gun and stepped out of the car, I could hear Raven shriek inside. I stood in front of the car waiting for whoever was inside to make their exit. When a man stepped out looking every bit like that little girl in the backseat, I opened both of their doors and helped them out. Sade's father stopped a few feet away. Her eyes lit up and she took off running. He picked her up and peppered kisses on her face. When he put her down his smile faded at Raven leaning against me. He approached us and Raven stepped forward. They embraced and I was bothered by that, but I played it cool. I had no place to be jealous.

"How are you?" He ran his hand down the back of her head. I involuntarily took a step forward, but Raven took a step back.

"I'm managing. Tariq this is Liam. He owns the security company that worked for my dad. He's also my friend."

"Friend? Friend vibes is the last thing that I'm getting from you two." He shook my hand.

"You're the one helping my baby with the guitar?"

"That's me. She's a natural. All she needed was to learn the basics." Tariq didn't respond but he was definitely posturing. He wanted Raven, based on his non-verbal behavior he might have had her recently or at least since they had Sade. He rubbed his chin and scratched the back of his head.

"Yo Ray, can I talk to you?"

"Nope, just take care of my baby." Raven bent in front of Sade and they embraced.

"Be good. I love you."

"I will. I love you too. Bye Mommy. Bye Mr. Liam."

"See you later, Sade."

"You will?" Tariq questioned.

"Boy bye! Come on, Liam." She practically purred my name and I bricked up instantly. I struggled to control myself. Raven was too close, but it wasn't the time. I didn't know if it would ever be the time again for us. She was still grieving, and I wasn't taking advantage of that. Right now, Raven needed a friend more than anything.

CHAPTER ELEVEN

 *Raven*

After picking up the barbeque chicken and green pepper pizza that I'd been craving, we headed back to the house. My sisters were lounging around on the front porch. They both refused to partake in the pizza, a satisfied smile formed on my face as I breezed into the house.

"You knew they wasn't going to eat that pizza, didn't you?"

"Yep! They don't think barbeque sauce belongs on pizza." I shrugged and tore into a slice after washing my hands. Liam watched me in what I could only describe as fascination.

"Come watch a movie with me and help me eat this pizza," I ordered with my mouth full.

"Give me a minute to check in with everyone. I'm going to relieve the crew. It will just be Leith and I after that." I watched Liam as he walked away. He walked with a purpose and exuded the right amount of confidence. It was natural for him; he wasn't trying. I shuddered from the memory of our first time.

"You're drooling a little, Sis." Ugh. I knew it was her house, but she just seemed to be around *all* the time.

"Oh, hey Angie." She stood there in front of me all tall, beautiful, and perfect. Her long jet-black hair was pulled up in a ponytail. Her features looked West Indian. Angie was dressed in short overalls and sneakers. The large frames on her face only added to her character. There was no good reason for me to give her the cold shoulder, so I decided to at least try to get to know her.

"What are you up to?"

"Oh, I was out back tending to my garden."

"You have a garden?" That piqued my interest since the most I'd done was grown herbs and flowers.

"Yep. I grow all of my own vegetables. It's definitely a money saver and healthier."

"I think that's cool. I'm great with flowers and I've been thinking about starting a garden. I keep a small herb garden in my kitchen at home."

"I can show you, if you like. I was planning to plant a few trees tomorrow morning if you want to join me."

"Okay. Thanks." I smiled. "Well, let me go set up this movie before Liam changes his mind."

"Don't tell me it's a romance movie." Angie cringed.

"A rom-com."

"Oh Lord! Good luck with that. I'll be in the lab if you need me."

I had no idea what that meant so I simply nodded. With a box of pizza in one hand and a couple of hard ciders under my arm I headed to the family room. I sat everything on the coffee table and scanned for a good movie. I settled on one of my favorite movies. Liam entered the room shortly after and studied the screen.

"What the hell is *Deliver Us from Eva*?"

"You're joking right...*Liam*. You've never heard of the movie?"

"No, I don't really do movies. I read a lot."

"Oh no, we can't have that. You don't know what you're missing and as a Black man you can't go around your people and not have seen the holy grail of black cinema." His eyes cut to me and the corner of his mouth turned up.

"Seriously, Ray?"

"Serious. Please tell me that you've seen *Coming to America*?" Wrinkles formed on his forehead and he played with the hair under his chin.

"Is that a slavery movie?" The laughed that burst through caused me to choke on my pizza. Liam stood up and patted my back until I could breathe again. The laughter would not stop as tears streamed down my cheeks.

"It ain't that funny," he mumbled.

"Oh my God. Aww I'm sorry. No, I'm not sorry but don't worry I got you." I don't know what rock he had been living under, but I made it my sole duty to bring him up to date on Black movie culture. With a wink I snuggled up against him and pressed the play button.

Liam actually enjoyed the movie and even laughed a few times. When he asked if I wanted to watch another one, I was more than happy to oblige. Near the end of the third movie, I woke up laying comfortably on Liam's hard chest, my arm draped across his torso.

"Wake up, Sleeping Beauty." His lips pressed into my forehead and I closed my eyes and smiled. We hadn't kissed or been intimate since our first time. He was being a gentleman and I appreciated that. There were nights where I wanted to go to him because I needed to feel something more than just the deep sadness that took over at night, but I didn't want him to judge me.

"I haven't been sleeping much. I guess having you here helped me to relax." My arms went over my head as I stretched my body. He didn't respond, but he held me tighter and kissed me on my forehead again. I took in his addictive scent and allowed sleep to claim me again.

The next morning, I woke up early, got a thirty-minute workout in and met Angie out back for my little gardening lesson. Angie had a mini farm. In her huge back yard, she grew all sorts of fruits and vegetables. I was impressed. She handed me a pair of gloves, a shovel, and shears.

"Okay so we will keep it simple. I'm going to plant a banana tree and two mango trees. You and I will do that together and I'll walk you through how to take care of a garden."

Angie knew her stuff and I was learning that she was a little bit of a nerd. She'd actually studied both botany and chemistry.

The girl made and sold her own soaps, body scrubs, lotions, and facial products. I was actually having a good time hanging out with her. My sisters were pretty much my only friends. One of my college roommates once told me that I gave off Jezebel energy. When I told her that it wasn't my fault if their men didn't want them after meeting me, she and any girl she knew stopped talking to me, so I kept to myself. It's been that way ever since, but Angie seemed cool and confident enough not to be threatened by me.

After we planted the trees, we harvested from her beautiful garden and she gave me a brief lesson on planting and growing crops. The back door slid open and Liam stepped out wearing relaxed fit jeans and a gray t-shirt.

"I see you two are getting along well, but I needed to steal Raven." He never took his eyes off of me while he spoke.

"What are you up to, Mr. Washington?

"Just a little lunch. Let's go." He held up a picnic basket. Usually, I didn't like being bossed around, but I liked it coming from him. I didn't get the impression that Liam did it to control me. It was just how he was. He didn't sugarcoat shit.

"Um okay. Just give me a minute while I help Angie with bringing the harvest inside."

"I'll get that. You take the blanket and find a spot."

"You got it. Thanks Angie. This was fun." I took off my gloves and washed my hands in the outside sink. She lifted a bucket of cucumbers and tomatoes.

"It was. I'm out here every morning. You can join me anytime."

"I'll bring mimosas next time," I spoke over my shoulder on my way to my favorite spot under the giant willow tree. I laid out the plush blanket and got comfortable. It was beautiful and quiet near the lake. I stretched my legs and planted my feet in the grass. The gentle breeze and the rustling of the trees were calming.

"You look peaceful." Liam's deep voice sent waves down my body. He sat next to me and began removing various items out of the basket. I sat up straight and helped him.

"Did you do this all by yourself?" I studied his features waiting for him to tell me a lie.

"Your sister's may have provided some input on your favorites."

"They know me very well."

We sat and talked while we enjoyed wine and a specially curated cheese plate of all my favorite things to eat. Well, I did most of the talking which was fine. Liam was definitely the strong silent type, but it worked. The wine had me extra relaxed with a blissful grin on my face that I couldn't get rid of. Even Liam loosened up and just enjoyed our time together.

My legs were draped across him and he began to massage my left foot. The gesture felt so intimate that I found it difficult to maintain eye contact. My eyes fluttered closed and my head fell back. Once he was finished with my right foot my entire body felt loose and relaxed. I read about how erotic a foot massage could be but never had the opportunity to experience it for myself. I mean I've had my toes sucked but I don't think that was the same, but if Liam even licked one of my toes, I was going to jump his bones right out here in the open.

Unable to help myself I sat up on my knees then kissed him. He sat still and allowed me to take my time. When he finally allowed me to slip my tongue between his full lips, I straddled him and moaned. He gripped what little bit of hair I had and held me in place while I explored his mouth. I felt Liam's attraction for me grow under my ass. We only stopped to come up for air. Both of our chests rising and falling. Our need for each other was undeniable. His hand caressed my face then he pressed his head against mine.

"Ray we shouldn't," Liam groaned.

"I know, but what we're doing is enough for now." His free hand played with the curls on the top of my head before he kissed my nose.

"Come on. I need to check in with Leith."

I couldn't help but feel like a slight wall was put up again, but

I was more than capable of breaking through it, so I didn't sweat it. I kissed him passionately before I climbed off of his lap.

"Thank you for lunch."

We walked up to the house then went our separate ways. After talking to Sade and checking in with my business, I headed straight for the shower. I had to give it to Angie. She put a lot of thought into these bathrooms. The one in my room was all white with black fixtures and greenery that was place strategically around the room. I laid back in the huge soaking tub and inhaled the scent of lavender from the diffuser. My peaceful bath was interrupted when the bathroom door flung open and my sister barged in.

"With my child being gone I thought I would be able to take a bath in peace. What do you want, Frick and Frack?"

"This seems to be the only way we can spend some time with you since you've been all up under Liam." Rayne pointed at me and hopped on the counter. I couldn't help but giggle. Liam could have all of my attention for as long as he wanted it. Aside from making my heart flutter and my lady parts do pirouettes, he made me feel safe.

"You really like him, don't you?" Rasheeda inquired.

"Yes, I do. I'm tired of just simply dating for the hell of it. With Liam I see what I could have with the right man and I want it more than anything." Neither of them spoke a word but I caught the looks they gave each other.

"Ut oh. What is it?"

"Nothing. It's just that we don't want you to get your feelings hurt. We are more familiar with Liam and he's always been so closed off, except with dad and now with you. Just make sure that he is taking you seriously and he's not just seeing you as someone who only wants to have fun."

"Damn, is that the energy I put out?" I sank down further in the tub when both of my sisters nodded. "What else am I supposed to do? I only know how to be me."

"And sweetie you don't need to be anything else, just make sure that your intentions are clear and that your actions match."

"I receive that. Thanks guys. Enough about me. What else is up?"

"Girl ain't shit. My fiancé and Rah's husband are about to send out an S.O.S if we don't get home soon."

"I had to convince the hubby that I hadn't taken the kids and left."

"Now brother in-law should know better than that. I am ready to go back to my normal life. I miss being at Self-Love and my cute little beach home."

"But Liam is in Highland City," Rah pointed out.

"True. I'm only a couple of hours away. We could make that work." I shrugged as I used the washcloth to rinse the soap off of me.

"We like him so don't screw this up."

"How would I do that?"

"By screwing Tariq," Rayne responded flippantly.

"Why can't we let the past be the past?" I pouted then stood up and wrapped myself in a soft bath sheet. The last serious relationship that I had ended because he caught me giving Tariq the ride of his life. That was about three years ago and the last time I was intimate with him. My actions had hurt someone that I truly loved, and it took me awhile to forgive myself. It also caused me to lose the friendship I was building with his sisters.

"Because that man has a way of getting in your head and in between your legs."

"Uh huh. Like muscle memory."

"Shut up, Rayne." I tried to keep a straight face, but we all ended up cackling.

"Let me get dressed so we can have a little happy hour."

"You look better Ray." Rasheeda acknowledged.

"I feel better. Of course, I'm still wrapping my mind around losing Dad but being here has helped me cope."

"You sure Liam ain't give you no more of that pipe?" My bestie wiggled her brows and rolled her hips.

"Raynnie shut up," Rah and I said in unison.

CHAPTER TWELVE

Liam

W e'd been at Angie's lake house for about a week now and although everyone had grown closer it was obvious that we were all growing restless. Raven and her sisters bickered about the smallest things. Leith and I just learned to stay away when they were going at it. The last time we intervene in one of their arguments they turned on us. I was ready to get back home to my solitude. Living in a house dominated by women was exhausting.

I'd been waiting on a phone call from Glitch and my second in command. When that call came, I asked everyone to meet in the living room. The sisters sat on opposite sides of the room. Today it appeared to be Rasheeda against Rayne and Raven. I rubbed the front of my head and Leith chuckled. Raven rolled her eyes.

"What is it, Liam? All this suspense is killing me."

"You were never the patient type."

"Who asked for your two cents, Rah?" Rayne snapped.

"Who made you Raven's spokesperson? You are always speaking for her."

"You're lucky she responded because you don't want to hear what I have to say."

"Say it, Raven! I dare you."

I whistled to silence the room. "Whoa ladies. Claws back in. I just heard back from my peoples and they got them ladies."

"The men who were responsible for killing Dad?" Rayne sat up in her seat.

"Yes. The last guy was apprehended this morning." Raven ran to me and jumped into my arms. I spun her around and squeezed her tight.

"Thank you. Thank you for everything." She kissed me on both my cheeks and then my chin. I kissed her on the lips and wiped away her tears with my thumb. After I put her down her sisters followed with thanking and hugging me and Leith.

"So that means we can go home? I love my sisters, but I miss my husband," Rasheeda inquired.

"Yes. We can all go home. I've made arrangements to head out tomorrow."

"I'm going to tell the girls we're going home and pack right now."

"I'm right behind you, Sis. Come on, Ray."

Before following her sister, Raven look back at me and mouthed thank you. Although it felt good to give them that news, my spirit was still unsettled. I couldn't help to think that there was more to it.

"You did it, Big Bro'." Leith embraced me and patted me on the back. I was only a few minutes older than him, but he was hell bent on claiming me as the older one.

"We did it. I couldn't have done this without your support."

"I'm here whenever you need me. You know that. So, you like this girl, don't you?"

"Yeah, I do. It's like she burrowed her way into me." *Into my heart.*

"What's next for the two of you?"

"I honestly don't know. We live in two different cities and I don't know how either of us will feel once things go back to normal."

"Word of advice. Don't pull a Liam and shut her out like you did Angie. Allow Raven to get to know the real you." Leith continued to sketch on a napkin while we talked.

"And scare her away? Nah." The corners of my mouth turned

down and I shook my head.

"You rather push her away?"

"I don't want to do that either."

"Then promise me that you will give her a chance to accept the man you are."

I simply nodded and dapped up my brother who wore a cunning smirk on his face. It was apparent that he took a liking to Raven and her sisters. He wasn't going to let this go. There was also the fact that Raven didn't seem like the type to give up easy. That just left me to make sure that I didn't stand in my own way.

After our celebratory dinner, I quietly snuck off to my room to have some much-needed alone time. I wasn't used to being in a house full of people anymore. It had been a long time since I lived like that. The light tapping on the door caused me to open my eyes and sit up in the bed. Angie poked her head in and grinned.

"Hey. Do you have a minute?"

"Yeah, what up?" Angie walked into the room and leaned against the wall near the window. She was dressed in a very thin nightgown. I raised an eyebrow.

"I was just getting use to you being around and now you're leaving." Her bottom lip poked out.

"Yeah. I still have a company to run and I need to do a little bit of digging into Gerald's assassination."

"You know you don't have to go. There is this thing called taking a vacation and I'm pretty sure you can use one." Angie was giving me a look that I knew all too well. I just had no idea where it was coming from.

She walked closer then sat on the bed where I sat reclined.

"Do you ever think about us?" That question caused me to frown.

"What do you mean?"

"I mean trying again. We were great together. The only problem was that you refused to open up to me. You can't deny we had great chemistry Liam."

Before I could form a response that wasn't going to ruin our friendship Angie crawled up the bed and straddled me. My dick betrayed me and reacted to her closeness. I cursed under my breath.

"Woah. Come on, seriously. Get up Angie." Her hands slid in my pants and I grabbed her wrist right before she grabbed me.

"Hey, Liam. Do you have a minute?" At the sound of Raven's voice, I pushed Angie off me. I didn't mean to, but I had no control of my reaction. She stumbled back. Luckily, I caught her by her arm and stopped her from falling on her ass. Raven stood there wide-eyed; her nostrils flared.

"What the hell are you doing?!" she yelled.

"Raven it was..."

"I'm talking to *her*. What the hell did I just walk in on?"

"Raven I'm sorry that you walked in on us. To be honest, that's none of your business. Liam is technically a single man."

"A single man who fucked me in my father's guest house before we came here. Several times I might add. Here I am thinking that we were cool and that we could potentially be friends and you're sneaking off trying to fuck him."

"Ray, no!"

Raven lunge towards Angie and I scooped her up. I didn't know if Raven could fight but I knew that Angie had been specially trained like me so she could probably take down Raven without throwing a punch. Raven bucked against me; she was stronger than I thought. Her sisters busted into the room and I just knew all hell was going to break loose.

"Ray what are you doing? Stop!" Rasheeda yelled.

"This bitch is up in here trying to fuck him."

"Raven that's enough!" my voice boomed. Raven's head whipped in my direction.

"Excuse me? Who are you talking to?"

Rasheeda stepped up before I could respond.

"Are you serious Raven? This is the last thing you should be worried about. First, we are guests in *her* house. Second, we just lost..."

"DON'T YOU DARE! Y'all always want to gang up on me. Never

on my side. You and Raynnie ain't loose shit! You both have a father who is alive and well. I have no one!" Her voice cracked and her bottom lip quivered. I reached to pull her in my arms, but she slapped my hands away.

"Don't touch me. You all can just leave me the hell alone. Fuck you, Angie!" Raven pushed passed everyone and stormed out of the room. Seconds later we heard her room door slam.

"Angie, I don't know what happened in here, but I want to apologize. Ray tends to self-destruct when she's hurting."

"Well, if you ask me, it sounds like Raven caught her pushing up on Liam. Everyone in this house knew there was something developing between them. From where I'm standing Raven had every right to pop off." Rayne's eyes stayed on Angie with every word she spoke.

"Oh, you would say that. You are always enabling her."

"Ladies." I cleared my throat.

"Sorry, Liam. We'll leave you two alone."

"The hell we will!" Rayne shrieked. She looked like she was ready to lunge at Angie next.

"Girl come on." Rasheeda yanked Rayne out of the room and closed the door. I spun around to face Angie. My eyes narrowed and my nostrils flared.

"What the hell was that?" I barked.

"That was me taking my shot. I've never stopped loving you and I couldn't just sit around watching you fall for her without making my feelings known. I still don't understand why we didn't work. I see you with her and she's like a train wreck in comparison to you, to us. Don't get me wrong, I like Raven. She's fun, impulsive, and outgoing..." Angie's words faded, and her face fell.

"Shit. She's everything that you need; exactly what you need, and I just messed things up. Liam I am so sorry. I didn't see it. I'll go talk to her. I'll make it right." I held my hands up to stop her.

"No. I think you've done enough."

"I'm sorry."

"I need space, Angie." I motioned my head towards the door.

"Can you just go?"

"Yeah, sure."

Once I was alone, I paced back and forth in front of the window. I would give Raven a minute, but she was going to have to see me tonight.

When I stormed into her room, she and Angie both yelped and jump.

"I thought I told you to leave her alone."

"I know I just needed to make it right."

"Get out, Angie," I gritted out. Her eyes glossed over and the look of hurt took over, but at the moment I didn't care. When Raven and I were alone I stood there silent, trying to control my anger.

"She apologized. Not sure if I can rock with her after what she did but at least she admitted that what she did was wrong."

"You can't go around jumping at people Raven."

"I can and I will if they try to take something that's mine."

"Oh. I'm yours?"

"Well yes and no." She shrugged and played with her nails.

"What does that mean Ray?"

"It means that we are not officially together, but something in my core tells me that you are mine. No one will get in the way of that. Unless you don't want..." She looked up at me with hope filled eyes. That look like she knew something I didn't.

"Honestly I don't know what I want." Raven jumped up and angrily poked me in the chest.

"Liar."

"Excuse me? And keep your hands to yourself." I spoke softly but my tone was serious. I didn't believe in putting my hands on women and that went both ways. Respect would always be given and expected.

"If that was true you wouldn't be in here to make things right."

"I just didn't want you thinking that I would do something so disrespectful to you."

Raven crossed her arms and stepped closer to me. "What do you want to do after we leave here?"

"I don't know. Maybe we should cool things down."

"Why so you can go fuck Angie with a clear conscious?" The venom in her words made my right eye twitch. Where the hell was she coming up with this shit? I had no idea, but she was poking the bear right now. I took a few deep breaths to steady my breathing and the pounding in my chest.

"If I wanted Angie then I wouldn't have devoted my time to you. I'm here with you."

"But you don't know what you want?"

"I don't Raven. I…" Raven released a rush of air before heading to the door and opening it up for me.

"Fine. When you know, then you know where to find me. If you don't mind, I would like to get some rest."

"Don't you think you are overreacting?"

"Get. Out. Liam." I was barely over the threshold when the door slammed in my face. This was not how I expected our last night here to go.

One month later…

It was a Friday afternoon and my dad had summoned his two sons over for dinner. I still hadn't made an appearance since arriving home from Palm Lake, so I was sure that he was feeling some type of way about that. I pulled in behind Leith's car and groaned. There was no doubt in my mind that he showed up early to make me look bad. He got a kick out of witnessing my dad rip me a new one. I let myself into the house and found them in the backyard grilling. Leith was manning the grill while my dad supervised and gave instruction. Lionel Washington thought he was the grill master, and truthfully, he kind of was. Dad could cook just about any meat to perfection. He pulled his *World's Greatest Dad* hat up a little and sized me up.

"'Bout time your ass made it over here to see your old man. I could be dead in my bed and no one would know it unless Leith showed up. Your brother stops by at least once a week. It's probably only to raid my pantry and eat, but he shows his face."

"I'm sorry Dad, and don't talk about dying like it's a joke." I looked my father dead in the eyes. My facial expression was serious along with my tone of voice.

"That was insensitive, Son. I know that the Senator's death is still fresh, but I need to see you more."

"Okay. I will do better and make the time."

"Good. That's all your father is asking for."

My dad pulled me into an embrace then patted me on the back. My brother and I performed our signature handshake.

"What up, Leith?"

"Ain't shit. I've been devoting more time to my art; working on a few new projects. I was commissioned to paint a mural at this holistic and wellness center in South Shores."

I gave my twin the side eye. The devious look on his face made me turn my body to give him my full attention again. He wanted me to know that he'd been in contact with Raven. I didn't know how to feel or what to think about that. She and I hadn't communicated since they were dropped off at Rasheeda's house after we left the lake.

"Since when did the two of you become so close?" My eyes narrowed.

"We spent weeks at that damn lake house what did you expect?" I didn't like what he was insinuating and felt my temper flaring up.

"I expect for you to know your place."

"Boys." My dad's tone held a warning.

"Know my place about what?" Leith frowned then a smile crept on his face. "I know what this is about. You…"

"Nigga you don't know shit!" I barked.

"I know that you are all in your feelings about Ray. What I don't know is why the fuck you're breathing down my back."

"Will you two shut the hell up!" Dad shoved a pan of ribs into my hands and slammed the top of the grill. "Over here fighting like some bitches." Leith and I remained still. My dad was pretty even keeled, and it took a lot to push him to this point. Seeing his sons fight could definitely push him over the edge.

"Damn, Dad. Tell us how you really feel."

"Yeah, chill old man before you have a stroke." The three of us broke into laughter as we followed my dad towards the house.

"Man bring y'all asses in this house. Makes me sick sometimes."

As we followed him into the house, I pulled Leith into a brotherly hug.

"My bad, Twin. I was bugging out there."

"Damn right. I'm not being sneaky, just keeping an eye on her until you come to your senses. She asked about you."

My attention was divided throughout dinner. I couldn't stop thinking about Raven. A month had passed since we all left Palm Lake and continued on with our separate lives. If I was honest with myself it was the longest month ever. A certain someone had indeed made a lasting impression on me and I missed her outgoing personality. Raven had somehow embedded herself into me and I refused to go another day without seeing her. I was craving her light.

The next day I found myself standing outside of Self-Love Holistic Wellness Center admiring its curb appeal. It was a white and grey standalone building with various succulents planted out front. When I stepped inside, I was greeted by a dark skin woman who was almost my height. She and what look to be two members all stared as I approached the counter. The place smelled good and was sleek and modern. When the receptionist didn't say anything, I spoke.

"Good afternoon. I'm here to see Ms. Jackson. Is she here?"

"May I ask who you are?" She looked me up and down then smiled.

"My name is Liam. Liam Washington. I'm a friend of the family."

"Just a friend?" The dark-skinned beauty donned a flirty grin.

"Nika why are you taking so long... Liam. Hey." Although she tried her best to mask it, I knew she was struggling to bite back a smile. There was no way I could hide mine. I wanted nothing more than to kiss those enticing and glossed lips. I pulled her close and wrapped her in a hug, which she returned.

"He *can* smile." I heard one of the lady's mumble.

"Hi Raven. You look good. How are you doing?" She did look good dressed in royal blue yoga shorts and a matching top. Her face was free of makeup and it made her look innocent, but I knew better.

"I am well. Thank you. I am wrapping up a class. I came down to get the oil that Nika was taking too long to bring. Nika, can I trust you to take Mr. Washington to my office?"

"Yes Raven." Nika rolled her eyes and smirked. "Follow me Mr. Washington."

"Make yourself comfortable. I'll be up as soon as I wrap this up." Raven called out.

Raven's office was a reflection of her, bright, airy, and colorful, with an earthy afro-centric flare. The walls showcased Black art and there were African figures placed on the table and bookshelf. After doing some work from my phone, I got caught up with looking at the various family pictures she had around her office. I was holding the picture that we all took at brunch when she walked in.

"Sorry, I didn't mean to impose." I placed the frame back in its place.

"No, it's cool. My dad meant a lot to you as well and I know daddy felt the same. Secretly I think he saw you as the boy he never had but always wanted."

"Mr. G was a good man." We were doing the thing I said I wasn't going to do and that was make small talk.

Taking off my jacket I slowly approached Raven.

"Are you hungry? Thirsty? Woah!"

My hungry mouth crashed into hers as I backed her against the door. We hungrily clawed at each other's clothes. I licked and sucked every piece of flesh that I could get my mouth on. Raven was quick to stick her hand into my sweats to release me. She pressed her small palm against my chest for me to step back before she kneeled in front of me and took me into her warm mouth. Her tongue twirled around my head before she deep throated as much as she could. I hissed and bit my bottom lip.

"Raven... Damn girl."

Her eyes closed and she moaned. The fact that she was enjoying herself so much would be my undoing. I cupped the back of her head and guided her motions. She was going to make me bust right down her throat if I didn't gain control. I stood back and slipped out of her mouth. Raven pouted and wiped her face with the back of her hand. She began removing her clothes and leaving a trail as she sauntered over to the navy-blue chaise lounge. I removed my shirt and stepped out of my sweats and boxers before I stalked behind her.

"Lay down," I commanded.

My face was in between her legs before she could get comfortable. My tongue licked and sucked on her clit. I wanted her first release to be quick but powerful. Raven held my head in place and wound her pelvis into my face. She dripped with arousal. I used my tongue to isolate her sensitive fleshed and flickered my tongue until she cried out in pleasure. She bucked and her back arched as she rode the wave to ecstasy.

"Yes, yes, yes." She chanted until she came down. I'd never needed to be inside of another woman more than I did right that moment. I crawled between her legs and pushed into her sticky center. Raven's arms looped around my neck and she wrapped her legs around my torso. Our eyes connected as I eased in and out of her feeling like this was the best pussy I'd ever had. Just as much as I was fucking Raven, she was fucking me back. She pulled me down and captured my mouth as we tongued and moaned into each other's mouth. I abruptly pulled back using one hand to hold her hands over her head and the other to squeeze her neck. I knew I was taking a risk but when Raven eyes rolled back, and she moaned I knew I'd met my match. My movements picked up and I pumped in and out of her slick folds. The sounds of our bodies slapping together, and our collective moans filled her office. If anybody walked by, they got an earful, but that was the last thing on either of our minds. Her body shuddered and she gasped for air as she orgasmed. Her pussy contracted around my dick sucking me in deeper, which was the end for me as I roared through my release. I moved in and out of her until I had nothing left. Raven held on until I was finished.

"Somebody was happy to see me." She sang. I smacked her on the side of her ass and kissed her.

"Happy ain't even the word, Baby. Raven. Raven, Baby, wake up. Don't you have work to do?"

"Huh? They can handle it, Baby. I'm the boss."

"Raven."

"Can you let me enjoy this after glow? Shut up and just lay here with me. You weren't worried about breaking me off in my office, but you're worried about me going back to work?"

Raven knew what she was doing. We laid there until my dick hardened again and she tilted her pelvis until I slipped in while I nuzzled her neck. I was in trouble.

CHAPTER THIRTEEN

A fter I taught my final class and left the next manager on duty in charge, Liam followed me home in his Ford truck. Why was I surprised that he owned a Ford? That was typical Liam; huge and reliable. I entered my code into the keypad to unlock my door and stepped inside. Liam followed and locked the door.

"Welcome to my humble abode." With a twirl, I guided him into my living room. My expensive gray couch sat against an emerald green accent wall. A beautiful art piece of a dark woman adorned in gold jewelry, framed by a gold sun and a red background with tribal print was hung in the middle of the wall. It was my favorite piece. It was a part of a series by an artist that I was obsessed with. The other two paintings were in my bedroom, I designed my home myself and was proud of the results.

"Aside from your property being directly on the beach, it is pretty humble."

Liam walked around the living area. He paid attention to pictures and artwork. I knew that I had a lot going on and a lot of stuff. I would describe my home as eclectic. It was decorated with souvenirs and art pieces from my travels.

"It's all about comfort for me. What do you think?"

"You have a lot of... stuff, but it's warm and inviting."

"Exactly what I was going for. What do you know any way? You probably live off grid in the woods somewhere or like a minimalist in a one room loft." Liam's eyes widened and he held his mouth open.

"I own both. I have a place in Harbor Creek, and I have my main residence in Highland City. It's loft style but has separate bedrooms."

"Harbor Creek? There's nothing there but a bunch of hiking trails and... well... trees." I scrunched up my nose. My bougie side was definitely rearing its pretty little head.

"All facts, but all of that equates to peace and quiet. A place where I can go to decompress and relax when I need to get away from the hustle and chaos of the city. Stop looking at me like that. It's a beautiful place, Ray."

"Hey if you say so. So, do you live in a cabin or tent?"

"You're a jokester now? Cute. It's a simple modest house."

"Okay. Maybe I'll get to see it one day." Liam grunted, but offered no formal invitation. Instead, he changed the subject.

"Where's Sade? School?"

"She's still with her dad. That means that she's doing virtual school." I sighed. Tariq and I fought over the best place for Sade to be. I wanted her back with me and he thought she needed some time away. On the contrary, I couldn't help but think that a part of him was doing this to get back at me. He could sense that there was something going on between me and Liam and he didn't like it. Sade had never met any of the men I was involved with, so I was sure that he did not like how comfortable his little girl was around Liam.

"Is everything alright? He frowned and moved closer.

"Yeah. It will be. Baby daddy is just being difficult right now, so I'll let him have his time."

We entered the kitchen and I cringed because it was still a mess from this morning, including the dishes I neglected to wash the night before. I moved around quickly putting dirty dishes into the dishwasher and wiping down the counters.

"Please excuse the mess. It's not normally like this." Liam simply nodded. I couldn't help but feel like I was in the middle of a home inspection and Liam was silently judging me. If he swipes his finger across any surface, then we were going to fight.

"Are you thirsty? I have hard cider, water, wine, apple juice, whiskey..."

"Truthfully? I'm still hungry." I was getting ready to run down what we could eat, but when Liam pressed his hardness against my back, and he kissed my neck, I understood exactly what he was still craving.

"Bedroom." His deep voice rumbled as he whispered in my hear. My entire body trembled in reaction. Verbally, I had nothing. Shit, what else was there to say? I slid past him then clutched his hand and led him upstairs where Liam took control of my body and sexed me until I felt like I had nothing left but, at the same time, had received everything. Liam was rough yet gentle. He knew when to dig in deep and when to pull back and kiss and caress me. He filled me up completely and massaged spots inside of me that I didn't know existed. His mind-numbing strokes erased everyman that I'd ever been with. Liam took claim over my body and I willingly handed it over. When he commanded me to come, my body jerked and released.

Sex with Liam energized me. While he laid with his eyes closed, I gave Liam my life story including my many hobbies, talents, and business ventures.

"You had perfect scores on your SATs?"

"Mmmhmm."

"And you play two instruments and are pretty much good at everything you do?" His fingers lazily grazed up and down my side.

"Yeah, I guess."

"Raven you're a genius you know that, right?" I pondered the thought then shook my head.

"You're the only one who thinks so. I mean, I think I'm smart as hell but a genius?"

"No, all jokes aside. You've never been tested as a kid?"

"Nope. My dad wanted to test me, but my mom wanted me

to have a normal childhood. She knew that my father was going to want to send me to the best schools even if that meant being away from home. Mommy wasn't having that."

We laid there silent but content. Usually when I slept with men, I was thinking of a way not to make an awkward exit or calculating how long they could keep my attention. Lying next to Liam, I was thinking everything but that. I was planning our wedding and what we would name the three additional children I would gladly give him. I was wondering what was on his mind and how he felt about me. Was this temporary for him? Was I just something fun to do? Were we just too different? A month had passed since we last talked then he just showed up to my job and fucked me senseless.

"So, is this what you came for?"

"What are you talking about?" he mumbled.

"This." I pointed between the two of us.

"Raven… One thing I need you to know about me is that I'm a grown ass man. If I only wanted sex from you then you would know. If I only wanted sex from you, I wouldn't have touched you since you're Mr. G's daughter. I'm not interested in just your body, Ray. To be frank, I'm not sure what this is, but I know that I'm interested in what's going on here, and here." He tapped my head and chest with his index finger. His hand rested on my stomach and I blushed.

"Mind, heart, and soul." I bit my bottom lip, kissed his chest then began to massage his dick back to life. He was about to have all his fantasies fulfilled off of that one. Liam's stomach growled, killing the moment and I giggled.

"Oh, my goodness. I'm such a bad host. Let me feed you."

"Can you make me your chicken and waffles?"

He held me tighter and punctuated each word with a kiss to my neck. Goosebumps prickled my skin. I loved it when he kissed me there. With a slick grin on my face, I turned around and straddled him. His big, calloused hands held me at my waist. I leaned forward and kissed him. After what he did to my body today Liam could have whatever the hell he wanted.

"Chicken and waffles coming up."

For the last four days Liam and I had been inseparable. These last few days with him were amazing. It was exactly what I needed. Liam had a calmness about him that kept me calm and grounded. I was always on ten, but his coolness kept me at a peppy six. His slow way of living slowed me down. Liam was happy doing the simplest things like taking a walk on the beach or reading a book while I binged watched reality TV. Today we were laid out in the family room. I was laying against him reading a steamy romance novel that had captured my attention for the last hour. Liam was on his phone checking emails and following up with his team. He gently kissed the top of my head before massaging my scalp, making me purr.

"Is that book really that good? Why do you read those things anyway?"

"First, romance is not *all* that I read. I have an extensive library in my office and on my e-reader. Second, yes, this book is *that* good. Reading romance books makes me feel good and fuels my hope that one day I too can experience that kind of love."

"How? What you're reading is fiction. Relationships take work and commitment."

"You make it sound like a job."

"It kind of is." I shook my head at his one-track response.

"But that's the problem. People don't want their relationships to feel like a job. Yes, successful relationships require you to work hard at it, but it's not a job. It's an experience. With your partner by your side, you can make it whatever you want it to be. I want romance, passion, affection, fun, and mind-blowing sex that prevents me from forming a complete sentence. I need to be loved like that. If I'm not getting what I want, then I have to communicate that and if that feels like work to whoever I'm with then we're not meant for each other."

Liam was quiet after that and I was worried that I might be scaring him away. I was self-aware enough to know that I could come on too strong. It wasn't in my nature to shy away from my feelings and sharing them.

"Read me something."

"Wha- what?" I scoffed.

"I'm still curious about what holds your attention so read to me."

"Okay!" I loved reading and never had a man to ask me to read to him, so I was ecstatic.

My finger was saving my place in my book, so I picked up where I left off. I cleared my throat and began to read. It wouldn't have surprised me if Liam had cut me off at some point and told me that he'd had enough but he never did. An hour later I closed the book because I needed to get ready. I needed to cover a class for an instructor who called out sick. I hated to leave Liam when he was going back home in the morning, but he reassured me that he'd be fine until I returned. Well, his actual words were, "Ray, I think I can manage without you for a couple of hours."

"Sorry to cut story time short but I need to change and head to work for a few."

I stood up and squealed when Liam pulled be back down on top of him.

"Liam!"

"I can see why you're so into those books." He kissed me on the lips and laughed when I relaxed against him.

"Nah, that's enough. Get up. I won't be the reason for you showing up late."

"Well, well, well. The boss lady has decided to grace us with her presence. I guess you finally decided to crawl from under that tall fine ass man who had these walls quaking three days ago."

My head fell in my palms. I shook my head and groaned.

"Oh, my goodness. Please don't tell me you heard us."

"Oh, but boss lady we did." Nika spoke in a seductive tone.

"How did we sound?" I looked up with a grin.

"Like he was breaking you in. Girl!" Nika fanned herself and we all laughed.

"Enough of fooling around. Let me go prep for this aerial yoga class."

I waved the girls off then floated over to my office. After placing my bag in my office and checking my messages, I made my way to the aerial studio. I selected my playlist of soft, soulful R&B then did a safety check on all the silks hanging from the ceiling. Closing my eyes, I swayed to the music and began to stretch out my limbs. Fooling around with Liam had me sore and stiff. We were opposites in so many ways, but his sexual appetite matched mine.

"Ugh I need to soak when I get home." I moaned. With a smile, I greeted the ladies as they slowly trickled into the room. I started the class with everyone sitting in their silks. We meditated then had a moment for vulnerability and gratitude. My center was a safe place for women so there was no comparison, no judgement, no gossiping, and no hating. This evening's class was exactly what I needed. Being around positive feminine energy always made me feel beautiful and sexy. I hung around after class to be available for any questions or feedback.

"Alright queens, I'm out. See you all tomorrow." The words tumbled out of my mouth as I blew passed everyone.

When I entered my home, I was greeted with the most amazing aroma. The combinations of vegetables, herbs, and spices had my mouth watering.

"Somebody's been busy. Wow!"

There was a trail of yellow flower petals leading up the stairs and also towards the back door. I followed the trail that led me outside. There was a table set for two on my screened in patio. I could hear the ocean waves crashing and smell the salty air. I took in a deep breath and released. Liam was lighting the last candle. He was dressed in jeans and a navy pocket tee. The left corner of his mouth turned up when he saw me.

"Just in time. How was class?" I met him halfway and we embraced then shared a passionate kissed like we weren't just laid up under each other on the couch a few hours ago.

"It was amazing. Too bad you couldn't sit in. It's an entire experience, but let's talk about this." I was cheesing so hard my face hurt.

"I wanted to do something special for you tonight before I head back home. It's hard for me to admit but I needed the time away. Thank you."

"You're a hard worker and I think you deserve more than four days. Thank you for coming. It was a pleasant surprise. I wasn't sure where we stood after that last night at the lake."

"I'm sorry about what I said. We can talk about that if we need to. Have a seat."

"No, let's consider this a fresh start. I feel like I'm under dressed. I should change."

"No, you're perfect."

Liam pulled out my chair for me to sit then took his seat across from me. A woman stepped through the French doors pushing a cart with drinks, salad, and appetizers. My eyes followed her as she placed everything on our table.

"Dinner will be served in about twenty minutes," she chirped before heading back into my house. I pointed my finger in her direction.

"Um who is she?"

"Chill. She's the private chef that I hired." Liam grabbed my hand, then kissed it.

"Okay. She's cute."

"That she is, but this feisty, short haired, sexy genius has my attention." My tongue traced my teeth as I fought to hide my smile. I rolled my eyes.

"Smooth, Mr. Washington. I am learning more and more about you, Sir."

"I hope you can handle what you learn." I was prepared to say something slick but the look on Liam's face led me to believe that his statement had a double meaning.

"I can handle more than you know."

We dined on Mediterranean cuisine while enjoying each other's company. The food was orgasmic. For appetizers we had Greek salad, hummus, and pita bread. Dinner included marinated chicken breast with grilled vegetables, roasted potatoes, and herb rice. For dessert we had a Greek-style apple pie. The sweet Red Blend wine had me feeling good and Liam's company didn't hurt either. After dinner we brought everything inside and I was led upstairs where Liam drew me a bath then ordered me to get naked which I happily obliged. The water was a perfect temperature.

"Hmm. This is exactly what I needed." I sank further into the tub.

Liam walked in free of any clothes. My eyes hungrily roamed over his body from top to bottom to... middle; it swayed like a pendulum. My man was blessed *beyond* measure, if you know what I mean. Yes, I said *my* man. There was no way he was going to be anything less than that. I prayed to God for this and I wasn't one to ruin an answered prayer. I was awarded with his sexy smile before he climbed in behind me. I lifted my phone from the tray in front of me and started my jazz playlist. Halfway through Coltrane, a Facetime call came in. I made sure that my face was in the frame before I swiped to answer.

"Hey, Baby!"

"Hey, Mommy! Guess what? Daddy took me to Disneyland and all the other parks. We had so much fun meeting all the characters and getting on the rides and eating good food. Daddy gave me money and I brought us matching glitter ears and tiaras." I smiled and listened as my daughter rambled on and on about her adventures in California. Sade's smile faded and her brow's furrowed before her eyes brightened up.

"Hey, Mr. Liam!" *Ah shit.* I fumbled with the phone and almost dropped it in the tub.

"Hey, Sade. Glad to hear that you're having fun." Liam replied although I had turned my body to get him out of frame.

"Mom why are you in the tub with Mr. Liam?" *Was that a smirk on my child's face?*

"WHAT!?" That was Tariq in the background.

"Honey Bun, Mommy will call you right back, okay? Love you!" I ended the call just as Tariq's face filled the screen. Liam chuckled before he pulled me into his embrace.

"Oops." He muttered into my ear before his tongue traced the outer edges. His hands began to roam my body as they moved down towards my center. As if on cue my legs spread on their own volition. His long fingers strummed against my bud pulling a deep moan out of me. Liam quickly worked me to my first of many orgasms for the night. My entire body felt like liquid and I was ready for more, but I needed to call my little girl back, so I bathed then wrapped myself in my white satin robe before I called her. It was good to hear her voice and to see her face. She was all the best parts of her father and I wrapped into one person. I still didn't know how her father and I were so lucky after the stunts we pulled. Before I hung up, I asked her to put her dad on the phone.

"Yo! Is that nigga..."

"None of your business. Look, I miss my baby. Have my child home next weekend. Don't make me have to come up there and get her."

"Nah, that ain't happening."

"Hmmph. I can always have a chat with your wife. I am really feeling like it's best that we confess all of our dirty sins and start with a clean slate." He didn't immediately respond but chose to glare at me.

"Fine. You play dirty, you know that?"

"Mama will do anything to get her baby home where she belongs. Don't fuck with me, Tariq."

"I love you too. We'll see you next Saturday." I gave him the middle finger and ended the call.

Liam was on the phone when I entered the room. He was standing on the balcony, but the door was open.

"Aye. Something is not right. You should have found out something by now. The reasons those men gave for killing Mr. G just doesn't make any damn sense. There has to be another motive. I usually feel settled after a job is complete and I don't."

"Excuse me. What are you talking about?" Liam spun around then cursed under his breath. He ended the call and reached for my hand. I moved back and crossed my arms. "No. I asked you a question." Liam rubbed his hands down his face. He shook his head.

"I don't want you worrying about this Ray."

"Tell me," I demanded.

"Capturing those men that killed you father seemed too easy, Baby. Allen said that the case was solved but their reasons don't make sense. It has to be someone else involved who conspired with them. The killer was a known hit man. Someone had to hire them. What I'm being told makes no sense. The evidence and statements just don't add up."

"Maybe the information is above your pay grade," I sassed. Liam narrowed his eyes and raised an eyebrow. I shrugged my shoulder. "What? Relax, Baby. It's over. They found my daddy's killer and him and the other men are all in jail. Just let it go." Something about my statement made Liam advert my eyes. I was about to get to the bottom of the things he wasn't saying but he spoke first.

"I don't know if I can let this go, but I don't want to discuss this tonight. Let me work through this."

"No. I want you to let this go, Liam."

"I'm not letting this go, Ray, so this conversation is over. Let's move on."

He brushed passed me and entered the bedroom. I followed. Tabling this conversation was the last thing I wanted to do, but I didn't want to end our time together arguing.

"Fine. Okay."

Liam and I spent the remainder of our time together making love and enjoying each other's company. He brought out feelings in me that I'd never felt. I thought I knew what love was when I met Tariq, but Liam was rewriting that definition for me and I prayed that I wasn't placing my heart in the wrong hands again.

Liam

Leaning against the door frame I watched Raven as she stood in front of the bathroom mirror and applied the finishing touches to her makeup. She glided the colorful lip gloss along her plump lips. What she was doing may have seemed normal, but it caused a reaction in me that had me shifting my stance. She looked beautiful in the burgundy V-neck dress that hugged every delicious curve of her body. Her hips swayed to the music playing from her Bluetooth speaker. Earlier that day her family and co-workers, along with my brother gathered together for a cookout in celebration of her birthday. All of the adults were continuing the celebration at a club. I wasn't excited about going out, so I told Leith to make sure he had his ass in the building too. He thought he was slick, but I caught him stealing glances at Rayne and grilling her fiancé Darryl. I'd have to talk to him about that. Leith liked the chase, but he would cut and run when it came time to settle down. Raven looked at me through the mirror and smiled. I approached her and handed her the unwrapped jewelry box in my hand. She spun around and leaned against the counter. Her eyes dazzled with excitement.

"What is this? You already gave me a gift, Baby."

"Open it." I urged.

She pulled the top up and gasped upon seeing the chocolate diamond tennis bracelet, "Oh my God Liam. It's gorgeous. Can you put it on?"

I took the bracelet from her and secured it on her wrist. The diamonds sparkled in the light and Raven wore the biggest grin on her face. She wrapped her arms around my neck, and softly pressed her lips into mine.

"I love it. Thank you."

"You look amazing, but do you have to leave your house in this dress?" I groaned in her ear. She expelled a husky giggle then pushed me back.

"I sure do because my ass looks good in this dress."

That was exactly why I wanted her ass to change, but Raven

Angel Jackson refused to be controlled and if I pushed it, she would only push back *and* win. Going back and forth over what a woman wears wasn't something that I wanted to involve myself with. I needed to focus on getting my head right for tonight. I didn't do large crowds.

When we entered the club, I found myself scanning the place. I made a mental note of all the exits. We were led to the VIP seating that sat about three feet higher than the dance floor. Raven was having the time of her life. She laughed and danced with her sisters and co-workers. It wasn't my scene, but we were all having a good time. That was until Raven was on her third drink and wanted to go on the dance floor. At that point the loud music was giving me a headache and I was ready to go, but it was her special day, so I obliged. The men led the women out to the dance floor. I stood off to the side while everyone danced. Raven swayed over to me and pulled me to dance. I shook my head.

"Ray, no. I don't dance."

"Come on, Liam. It's my birthday. Are you going to tell the birthday girl no?" Raven turned with her back facing me and began to grind against me. Her happiness was contagious, and I eventually began to move with her. Besides, what self-respecting man just stands there like a lame while his woman is seductively rolling her ass up against his manhood? Raven turned and looked at me in surprise. I said that I didn't dance, not that I couldn't. This wasn't so bad. Raven stepped back and danced for me like we were the only two in the room. I enjoyed her performance and nodded to the music. When some random dude walked up on her and started grinding on her ass, I instantly saw red. By the time I blinked the guy was on the ground holding his face and Leith is working his way to me.

"What is wrong with you?" Raven yells over the music.

"More than you know and can handle." My tone was deadly. Raven's expression softened.

"That's not how I meant it and what does that even mean anyway? I just meant that you have been acting strange since we got here." Raven grabbed my hand and I pulled away. The last thing

I wanted was to be touched. It felt like the walls were closing in on me. I needed to get out of here. A hand rested on my shoulder and I cocked my fist back.

"Whoa! It's just me bro." Liam held his hands up. "Are you good?"

"Nah, I need to get the hell out of here. Come on, Ray. Tell everyone goodbye so we can leave."

"Liam…" I tuned her out and led her back to our section so she could say goodbye. We grab her purse and she promised to let her sisters know when we made it back home in one piece. The ride across town was quiet. I knew Raven probably had questions; I was praying that she didn't ask them. Not sure if she was nervous or aggravated but she kept tapping her nails on her purse. The shit was grating my nerves.

"Will you stop that please?"

She threw her hands up and released a rush of air. "Are you going to tell me what that was about or are you going to continue being a damn grouch?"

"He was being disrespectful. Disrespectful to me but most of all to you. Did you give him permission to touch you?"

"No, but…"

"Did you enjoy his hands on you?"

"Of course not." She rolled them damn eyes.

"Exactly. My job is to protect you. You don't ever have to worry about that shit when I'm around."

"And I appreciate that. I have no doubt that you can and will always protect me, but it's not your job."

"It's my job when your mine." That admission gave both of us pause. Raven shifted in her seat and turned towards me. I glanced at her before focusing back on the road ahead of me.

"That back at the club was a lot. It seemed to be more than about protecting me."

"That back there was nothing Ray. I've done worse than that. If you can't handle that then you can't handle me."

"So now I can't handle you?" Raven's eyes narrowed and she bit down on her bottom lip. She released her seatbelt then began to unbutton my pants.

"Ray, Baby, what are you doing?" She reached inside my pants and pulled me out. With a lick of her hand, she began to stroke my shaft. My member swelled under her ministrations and I groaned. Just like that, I forgot about my anger and anxiety. How quickly my mood changed.

"What does it look like? I'm showing you just how much I can handle you, Mr. Washington." She teased my head with her tongue before she took me all the way in. I fought the urge to close my eyes. There was precious cargo with me so I couldn't afford to wreck out. Keeping my right hand on the steering wheel I used my left hand to ease the seat back to give Raven room to work her magic. This shit was insane. In just a couple of minutes I was shooting my load down her throat. The view of her licking me clean had my head spinning, but in the best way possible.

CHAPTER FOURTEEN

Liam

Not sure how she did it but I'm pretty sure I was Raven Jackson's boyfriend. Since reconnecting we'd been traveling back and forth visiting each other. She'd spent several weekends at my place and Sade had come a few times as well. I grew to look forward to the weekends, so I made sure that I always had them off when possible. We'd form a routine that was easy and light. Initially, I had to get used to having Raven around. Whenever she would visit, my sink that was typically bare because I kept everything in the cabinets and drawers, would be filled with makeup, perfume, soaps and jewelry. She would leave blankets and cardigans scattered all over the place because she was always complaining that she was cold. In the beginning it used to drive me crazy to the point where we would argue about it, but I had grown accustomed to it, almost. Sade was having a sleep over with her cousins, so Raven was going to stay with me.

Taking a break from my morning jog, I stopped at the pull up station and did three reps of twenty. It was seventy degrees and Christmas was two weeks away, not that I cared but Raven and Sade couldn't stop talking about it. They'd even called themselves surprising me by buying me a Christmas tree and decorating it. It was black, silver, and red to accommodate my taste, so I was rocking with it. My phone vibrated and I tapped my ear pod to answer.

"Liam Washington."

"Hello Liam Washington. This is your better half Leith Washington." My brother mocked me.

"What up Leith?"

"I'm at your house where you at? You still out running?"

"Yeah, but I'm on my way back. Let yourself in."

"Already at the door. Holy shit! Is that a fuckin' Christmas tree? Why does it smell like cinnamon in this bitch?"

I sucked my teeth and ended the call before hightailing it back to my house. There were signs of Raven all over the place and I knew the tree was going to tempt Leith play investigator and go through my shit. When I got home, I came across my neighbor who was struggling with her groceries, so I help her carry them to her door. I ignored her invite to join her inside before jogging to my unit.

"Yo, Leith," I called out.

"Dawg. You got all the good shit in your fridge. Who's been shopping for you because all you do is eat meat, vegetables, boiled eggs, and smoothies. Oh, and I found these in your drawer."

While chugging a bottle of water I looked over at Leith on my couch eating a sandwich. He was waving a pair of yellow lace thongs that undoubtably belonged to Ray.

"Man, if you don't get your damn hands off of her underwear. Why are you going through my shit? Creep." I approached the couch and snatched the delicate piece of underwear from him. Leith laughed and took a huge bite out of his sandwich.

"Her as in Raven?"

"Who else?"

"Good point because only Raven could get your ass to put up a tree. Dad would be impressed."

"He's seen it and now he's been pushing to meet her."

"Word? Y'all at meet the parent stage already?"

"Her family knows me, and I was close to her dad, so it only seems fair. All I have is you and dad and you two have met."

"Yeah, and don't forget my kids and Angie."

"Don't remind me of Angie." I groaned. Angie and I have spoken a few times since the incident at her house, but it was always awkward as hell. It felt like we'd lost that connection that made us friends.

"Truth be told I think Raven could have taken Angie. I could hear her mouth all the way from the kitchen that night."

"Do you know she and Angie talk on the phone?"

"Damn." Leith shrugged. I shook my head because he was already uninterested in the conversation.

"I'll be back. I'm going to shower." My twin simply grunted and turned my TV to ESPN.

Once the steamed filled the bathroom I stepped to the shower and let the hot water loosen up my muscles. I closed my eyes and allowed the water to run down my head. I must have bumped my arm into the shelf because a few bottles of shampoo and body wash tumbled to the floor creating a raucous that disturbed my calm. A scene of gunfire and death flashed in my head and my eyes popped open. I braced the wall and struggled to take deep breaths to prevent the onslaught of a panic attack. I hadn't experienced flashbacks in years, and it scared the hell out of me. I turned the water off then stepped out of the shower. After counting down from one hundred I freshened up and got dressed. The terrifying experience left me feeling weak, so I took a seat on the side of my king-sized bed.

"Bruh, you alright?" My body stiffened. I clenched my hands into fists to stop them from trembling. I looked up to see concern etched on my brother's face; it was like looking in a mirror. There was no use lying to him because he would know. We always knew when something was wrong with the other. It's difficult to explain but we would get this sick feeling in our stomachs. While I was away in the Marines Leith struggled with sleeping and nightmares. To cope he relied on getting high and experimented with some hardcore shit, but we were both fighters so together we overcame our demons.

"I can't stand being a twin sometimes," I mumbled.

"I heard that. What's up?"

"While I was in the shower, I think I had a flashback." I pushed out as I stood up from the bed. My legs were still shaky.

"Damn bruh. Do you know what triggered it? Does old girl know about them?"

"No and no. Never had a reason to tell her." Leith squinted his eyes, and I knew he had more to say. A conversation that I wasn't in the mood to have.

"Don't you think you should tell her?" Instead of responding I chose to ignore him. I smoothed out my bed from where I'd been sitting. He got the hint.

"Welp, come on. We ain't got to talk about shit. Let me fix you a drink and get you high as fuck."

"I'm not smoking. Raven gets in today."

"It helps your anxiety. I'm sure Raven won't care. We both saw how she and her sisters get down. She'll probably smoke with you."

"Nah. I'll pass, but I will have that drink."

Leith hung around for the rest of the morning and into the afternoon. It'd been a minute since we chilled like that. The two of us just hanging out talking shit. Leith always had a story about some crazy woman he was dealing with or shit that went down while he was traveling. He was always attending or holding events to showcase his artwork and met all sorts of people. I'd missed the last few events, so I made a mental note to attend the next one.

"My next event is the week of Christmas. You coming?"

I looked over at him, smirked, then nodded my head. "Most definitely. I'll see if Raven wants to come."

"Bet."

Both of our heads turned when the sound of keys jingling slapped against the door. The alarm beeped and announced that the door had been opened. The sound of wheels and heels echoed, and the smell of jasmine vanilla and cocoa butter permeated the room, then there she was. Raven came into view beaming and looking absolutely gorgeous. My place instantly felt warmer. She was wearing a burnt orange V-neck top, jeans, and brown boots that reached her thighs. Personally, I thought the outfit was a little too warm for today's weather, but Raven did live on the coast so she may have left cooler weather and didn't bother to change before leaving. I was already up from where I sat on the couch and was moving towards her. She dropped her bags and leaped into my arms.

"Hey, Baby!" As soon as her lips pressed into mine her tongue snaked into my mouth. I wasn't big on public displays of affection, but I wasn't going to refuse her. Leith cleared his throat.

"Oh, hey Leith." Raven seductively chewed her bottom lip and slid down my tall frame. It was obvious that she felt my body's reaction to her being in my arms. She went and hugged my brother and playfully shook his arm.

"Did you take that advice that I gave you?"

"Uhh." Leith looked down and rubbed the back of his head.

"About the CBD oil?" Raven quickly corrected, avoiding whatever it was Leith didn't want me to know. Now these two were covering up something.

"CBD oil? Seriously? You and my brother talk?"

"Uhh yeah. From time to time we still check in." Raven fidgeted under my gaze. She was a horrible liar and definitely couldn't lie to the people she cared about.

"Ugh! He asked for advice about a girl now stop interrogating me. I've had a long morning I'm going to shower and change." Raven avoided looking a Leith whose eyes narrowed in her direction.

"I knew something was different about you. Who is she?" I smiled and crossed my arms across my chest.

Leith grabbed his keys and phone and shook his head. "I don't know what you're talking about bro'. I need to go. Gotta finish up this piece I'm working on."

"Yeah, okay. You do know I have my ways of finding shit out."

"Don't even think about it." Leith laughed. We hugged and he saw himself out. Yeah, someone had definitely caught his attention. While Raven showered, I swiped through my phone in search of what to order for a late lunch. I knew Raven would be hungry but wouldn't want to go out so soon. She loved pizza from the mom-and-pop Italian restaurant a few blocks over, so I ordered a couple of pizza's and a salad. Raven came down the stairs in her purple fuzzy slippers and a matching two-piece set. The sides of her head were shaved with a flower design on her right side.

"You cut your hair."

"Mmmhmm. Just a little. I like to switch it up a bit." She rubbed her hand over her hair then curled up on my couch. I sat next to her then lifted her onto my lap.

"I ordered from Antonio's."

"How did you know? I've been craving their food all day." Raven danced in my lap and I curved my lips upward. She stopped and stared at me. Her hand caressed the scar on my face.

"How are you? Is everything okay?" I made an attempt to divert my eyes, but she held my face. Raven had a knack for reading people, myself included, but I didn't know how to have that conversation with her.

"Don't worry about me. I'm okay."

"It doesn't feel like you are, Liam." My intercom dinged and I knew it was the food. I tapped Raven's thigh. She sucked her teeth and rolled her eyes before getting up. I went to the screen and pressed the button to grant the delivery guy entrance to the building. Raven moved past me and into the kitchen to grab plates, napkins, and placed them on the table. She then moved to the fridge and grabbed a beer for me and a bottle of wine for her. I tipped the driver and sat the food on the table. I watched as Raven moved around fixing our plates. Doing it all while pouting. She did a quick blessing over the food and went for a slice of pizza. I intercepted her hand. She gave me those big, gorgeous eyes.

"Look. There are things about me that you don't know about. I've been through a lot of crazy shit; things that I'm still working through."

"And you're not ready to open up to me about that part of

you."

"No, I'm not."

Raven sighed and reached for the pizza. "I don't like hearing that, but I have to respect it." This visit was going in the wrong direction. Raven was emotional and negative feelings tended to weigh her down until she fell into a funk that was hard to pull her out of. I needed to do something and fast.

"Spend Christmas with me and my family; you and Sade."

"Really? Your family?"

"Me, my dad, and Leith."

"You- you want me to meet your dad?" Her eyes lit up and she smiled.

"Yes, and he's eager to meet the woman that has his son unrecognizable. His words not mine."

"I would love to." She stabbed at her salad and shoved a forkful into her mouth. She spoke with caution. "Can you tell me about him?"

"Sure. My father was everything me and my brother needed. When I was ten my mother was in a car accident and suffered a traumatic brain injury. She was never the same after that. She would get these angry spells when she would black out and trash the house or beat the shit out of me and Leith. My last time seeing her she was in a rage, tearing up the house and then everything went black. She had attacked Leith and I stepped in the help. I hit my head and suffered a concussion. My dad said that she told him that we were better off without her. That night when my dad got home from the hospital she was gone. At first, he waited for her to return and it was like we were frozen in time. Eventually it began to take a toll on us in different ways. I withdrew emotionally and lashed out whenever I felt cornered. Leith was wildin' out in school. My dad realized that he was at a critical point and in the beginning stage of losing his sons. He knew than that he had to step up and move forward. One night during dinner he explained everything to us and told us to get our shit together because after this conversation he was whooping ass." I smiled at the memory and Raven giggled.

"Lionel Washington never missed a school production, awards ceremony, game, or graduation. There were times I forgot that I had a mom. He was that great of a father. All the kids in the neighborhood loved him and looked up to him as the neighborhood dad."

"He sounds like an amazing man. I hope he likes me."

"Mr. G reminds me of my dad. They had similar personalities. You two will get along fine. I'm not worried about that."

"Thank you for sharing a piece of you. I know that's not easy for you." Raven leaned over and pecked me on the cheek.

I wanted to argue that wasn't the case, but that would have been a lie. She was right. Opening up about the shit that I've done and seen wasn't something that I liked to do. It was something I wasn't sure if I wanted to do with Raven. She would look at me differently if she knew the real me. The darkness I kept hidden would snuff out her light. I would protect that at all costs.

"It's just that you are such a loner, Liam. Other than work, Leith, and me you spend your time here or in the woods alone. I just want more for you. I want you to be happy."

"I like being alone. It doesn't bother me, and I don't feel like I'm missing out. Plus, you make me happy. The people I have in my life are enough. It's best that way." Raven sat her pizza down and wiped her hands. She had that inquisitive look in her eyes.

"What does that mean?"

"It simply means that my lifestyle works for me. It keeps me centered and sane. Peace and tranquility are what I need."

"Is that why I don't hear from you for a few days after we always part ways?" *Dammit*. I walked into that one.

"Truthfully, yes that's why and it's not a bad thing. You're so extroverted and full of energy. After our time together I do need the time to decompress and just be to myself."

What I wasn't saying was that Raven's energy was sometimes all over the place, and that it made me anxious. Recently she had been adjusting to my lifestyle and was showing what I called her yogi side. That was when she gave off soothing energy that kept me calm. Raven didn't seem to take offense of my admission. She took a sip of wine before finishing off her third slice of pizza.

"My momma used to tell me that my light was bright. Brighter than most people. So bright that it could make other's jealous or feel overlooked. She told me to never dim my light for fear of other's reaction but never shine so bright that I blocked out those that mean the most to me. I didn't understand her last statement but now I think that she was telling me to shine but humble myself. I say that to say, I know that I am a lot sometimes and I know that our personalities are completely different. I just need for you to tell me. I don't do well with rejection. It feels a lot like abandonment. Now that I know, I don't have to go down the rabbit hole of all the possible reasons why I haven't heard from you."

"Reason's like what?" I asked with a mouth full of pizza.

"You know the usual, you've grown bored with me or I'm not the only woman that you're dealing with." She shrugged like it was nothing, but her last statement was spoken like a question. I didn't want Raven to question her position and I didn't want her to think that I was that type of man.

"There's no one else but you Ray."

"Thank God because the thought of any heffa getting even half of what you're dishing out in the bedroom makes me want to cut a bitch."

We both laughed at her admission. After dinner we went for a walk by the lake then went at it in the shower. I couldn't get enough of Raven. It was like a thirst I couldn't quench. She always left me both fulfilled and wanting more.

CHAPTER FIFTEEN

We were in my favorite lingerie store Silks and Satin. I was looking for something sexy to help wish my man a Merry Christmas. The morning was spent on last minute Christmas shopping. The mall was our final stop and we'd already explored almost every store. I stepped out of the dressing room wearing a wine-colored lace one piece. The material felt butter soft and it looked amazing on my skin.

"Yassss, Sis! It's makes your ass look good. Now that just might get you pregnant."

"She's right. Make sure he wraps it up."

"Seriously Rah?" I groaned then giggled.

"Yes. This thing between the two of you is still new. Kids would just confuse and complicate things."

"This hurts me to say this but you're right. Besides, I don't even think I can get pregnant again. After a few other slipups we got tested and stopped using condoms. As much as we get it in, I should be pregnant by now."

Although I wasn't trying to get pregnant, it didn't go unnoticed that I hadn't had not one pregnancy scare. *That* scared me. I wanted more children someday. How would Liam feel if I couldn't conceive? Does he even want kids?

"Nope. Get out of your head, Ray. It's just not the right time."

Rayne squeezed my hand. "Now go change so we can get out of here. I'm hungry." She and Rayne laughed as I was shoved back into the dressing room."

After dropping off the gifts to Rayne's house, we headed to our favorite restaurant for food and drinks. As always, we feasted on all of our favorite appetizers. The popular spot was originally a house that was converted into a restaurant. We ate here so much that everyone knew us and our orders. I was munching on a conch fritter which was the most popular item on the menu. My phone dinged, alerting me that I had a message. It was a text from Liam. I smiled at his message and quickly replied back.

"Raven if that is Liam tell him that you are having sister time right now. He can have you later."

I mumbled, "Hater," then dropped my phone back into my purse. "What's the tea ladies?"

"Your old boyfriend from high school moved back in town."

"Next!" I yelled and we all laughed. I used to think I was so in love with that boy. He had me doing everything I wasn't supposed to do then he dumped me for the guy who I thought was his best friend. Imagine being sixteen and catching your boyfriend sucking dick. To get revenge my sisters and I did some unspeakable things to his car. Things that I was not proud of.

"We promised to never bring him up again."

"Woo child! When you called me and Rayne crying and yelling about Peter sucking dick…"

"Yeah, you two did exactly what you all are doing now. Laughed."

"Aww we're sorry Ray. My sweet little sister." Rasheeda leaned across the table and pinched my cheek. "Okay, let's talk about something important. Are you coming home for Christmas?"

"Yeah, I was thinking that I would spend the morning with the family them spend time with Liam and his family."

"Great! Raynnie and I was talking, and we thought that it would be a good idea if we spend Christmas at the estate."

My body tensed and I released a frustrated sigh. "I'm not feeling that idea."

"Why are you avoiding going back to the house? You were raised there."

Rayne looked at Rasheeda as if she was saying, *I told you so.* Rah rolled her eyes. Choosing not to respond I took a sip of my Dark and Stormy then popped a cheese fry in my mouth.

"Ray. Did you hear Rah?"

"Look. I'm not ready to go back there. It's too hard."

"Life is hard Ray. It's time that you stop running from the hard shit. You won't have to do it alone sis. Rayne and I will come with you. You are in charge of the estate now. Don't neglect your responsibilities."

"Rah, drop it," I snapped. "Please."

"Fine. It's not my intention to upset you and I apologize if it did."

"It's cool." I'd shut down on my sisters. I didn't like thinking about my dad or the state of my childhood home. Whenever the subject came up my mind was riddled with memories of what happened that day. I didn't want to be pressured into doing anything before I was ready. The conversation was a mood killer, so we cut our time short. Rasheeda went home to her family and I stayed with Rayne at her house. As soon as I was settled, I checked in with Liam.

"Ray."

"Hey Liam."

"Is everything all right? You don't sound good."

"You know my sisters and I can't go a whole day together. It gets draining. I'm just tired, but I wanted to hear your voice before I go to bed."

"I wouldn't have minded if you would have stayed here with me."

"I know, but Rayne mentioned me spending more time with you and less with them so I'm hanging around. You will definitely see me tomorrow."

"Good. We can drive to the woods as you call it. I think you could use some fresh air."

"Maybe you are right. I can't wait."

"Get some rest. I'll see you tomorrow."

"It's a date. Goodnight."

After I had enough sister time, Liam scooped me up the next morning and we headed to Harbor Creek, aka, the woods. All jokes aside, his place was really nice. It was a modern style modular home. It was made from a mixture of wood and steel shipping containers, so it stood out from all the other cabin style homes we passed on the way up. Liam was living off grid and the home was powered through solar panels and some other high-tech hookup he tried to explain to me. The property was beautiful, and I instantly fell in love. I'd enjoyed my time there more than I expected to. The fresh clean air and the stillness was exactly what I needed. Liam took me on a hike and then taught me how to fish. He taught me all about how to survive in the wilderness and was so serious about it. I giggled the entire time until he gave up and we retired inside his home for dinner on the deck. Cooking with Liam felt natural and he turned out to be a pretty good cook. Every minute we spent together I learned something new about him. It was like putting together a puzzle. This was my first healthy relationship, and I cherished every moment with this incredible man. He didn't grasp how special he was or how much he'd taught me. I couldn't wait to make more memories with him. Christmas was going to be great.

CHAPTER SIXTEEN

Liam

Raven was late and not by a forgivable amount of time. She was supposed to be here almost three hours ago. I went from annoyed, to worried, and then to angry. I could deal with Ray being late for dates with me or even her birthday for that matter, but to flake on my family, my dad. The shit was just disrespectful. She and I hadn't spoken since we Facetimed each other this morning. Raven was bare face and beautiful while Sade bounced around in the background, excited to open her presents. I smiled at the memory then shook my head.

"Son that girl got your emotions all over the place. You don't know how to feel."

"Dad this is unacceptable. I- I'm sorry."

"Relax Liam. Something could have happened. Try calling her again."

"I did and it's going to voicemail. I need a drink," I mumbled to myself. I stood up from where I sat on the couch and stretched my limbs before I walked over to the wet bar.

"Get me a drink while you're up, Son."

"Me too," Leith added.

"Y'all ain't shit." I chuckled. They were so focused on the TV that neither responded. Lights from a car caught my attention. Through the window I could see Raven's black Jeep in the driveway.

Before I walked outside, I heard Leith yell, "Show time!"

I met Raven at her car and helped her out. She smiled and wrapped her arms around my neck and my body tensed.

"Hey, Baby! Merry Christmas."

"You're late." I turned my head to avoid her lips landing against mine. Raven's smile faded and her eyes held questions.

"Yeah, I ran into traffic and lost track of time at Rah's house."

"Whatever Ray. It's windy as hell. Let's get you two inside."

"Liam I'm sorry." Moving past her I opened the back door. I bent down and smiled.

"Hey little lady. Merry Christmas."

"Merry Christmas, Mr. Liam!" Sade climbed out of the car and jumped in my arms. After I adjusted her in my arms, I made my way towards the house. Raven trailed behind.

"Come on. We were just getting ready to sit down and eat."

"Well, well. If it ain't Ray Ban and her mini me. You finally decided to grace us with your presence." Raven and Leith hugged, and I noticed her give him a look of warning as she shook her head."

"What's up Leith."

"This *is* a Merry Christmas. Did Santa come back and drop off these two beauties?" Leith groaned and I rolled my eyes. My hand rested at the small of Raven's back.

"Dad this is Raven Jackson and her daughter Sade. Raven this is my dad."

"I'm pleased to meet you Mr. Washington." Raven pulled my dad into a hug. He was pleasantly surprised.

"You're strong pretty lady!"

"Raven owns a wellness and fitness center. She's a personal trainer among other things."

"Mr. Washington, I want to apologize for my tardiness." My dad waved her off and led us all to the dining room.

"Nobody's worried about that except that tight ass son of mine. He went from a bad ass to a stiff ass. Always so serious. I tell him all the time that he needs to relax and enjoy life. From what I know it seems like he's doing that with you."

"I try my best. I'm sure my carefree attitude drives him crazy sometimes." Raven was trying to get me to talk to her, but I could not get over being upset about her being so damn late. She was supposed to be here hours ago. I assisted her and Sade with their seats and sat across from Raven. Dad said grace and we all dug in. Raven and my dad talked about everything under the sun. My dad was a talker whereas I wasn't, and Leith was always distracted so I knew that he would love Raven. She just had a way with people, but her charm wasn't working on me tonight.

"Mommy you forgot something."

"That's right. Sade and I brought presents for everyone."

"We opened presents hours ago Raven, but of course you wouldn't know that because you were..."

"With my family," she gritted. Her fork hit her plate with a loud clang.

"Can we speak in private please? Excuse me, Mr. Washington." Raven got up and headed towards the front room without waiting for my response.

"Ooo you're in trouble Mr. Liam," Sade sang.

"Hush and stay out of grown folks business little girl!" Raven yelled from the front of the house.

My dad loved Christmas, so the entire front room was decorated. The room looked like Christmas blew up. Raven waited for me near the picture window with her arms crossed.

"First your late, then you want to interrupt dinner to do what, Ray? Argue?"

That's just it, Liam. I am not trying to argue with you, but you're acting like you're just itching for a fight. I apologized for being late. It will never happen again. No one else seemed bothered by it but you."

"You're late all of the time, Raven."

"Maybe I am but I am *trying*. This is our first holiday without Daddy. I didn't even want to get up this morning. It took all of my energy to put on this happy face for my sweet child who still believes in Santa and you will do the same. Yes, I got caught up and lost track of time with my sisters and their family. I'm doing the best I can do today, and I won't stay here another minute if you're going to waste the rest of today reminding me that I screwed up. I know that I'm not your ideal woman…" Raven was talking herself into a holiday meltdown and I needed to repair the damage. I didn't want to fight. Not on today of all days.

"Hey, stop. Baby I'm a jerk. You needed to be around your family today. I'm sorry for the cold attitude. I don't do well when things don't go the way I planned it. The entire day had been meticulously planned out in my head and I just wanted it to be perfect."

"It can still be perfect even if it doesn't go *your* way. We're here now. Let's enjoy the moment. I've missed you." Raven's hands slid up my chest. I bent down and sucked her bottom lip into my mouth. My hands moved down Raven's back and clutched her ass, allowing her to feel the affect she had on me. She moaned into my mouth. We needed to stop before I took her upstairs and had my way with her in my childhood bedroom.

"Bruh stop feeling up on my sister by the Christmas tree. Dad sent me to make sure it was safe to come out."

"They better not be out there being fresh!" Dad yelled from the dining room, but I could hear the amusement in his voice.

"They were Dad." I shoved Leith and Raven giggled.

"Can you help me get the gifts out of the car?" I planted soft pecks on her neck before releasing her. Sade came skipping into the living room with my dad. He handed her a plate with a small slice of cake when she found her place on the couch. After Raven passed out our gifts, I pulled her onto my lap. She'd done a great job with choosing the right gifts. She gifted Leith with new art supplies and my dad with whiskey made by a Black-owned company. Leith, my dad, and I hadn't celebrated the holidays together in about three years. It was hard because I was buried in my work and Leith was traveling the world and engaging in all sorts of debauchery at the time. Sitting here with my arms wrapped around Raven and watching her laugh and joke with my dad and brother felt good. After drinking eggnog and watching Christmas movies we said our goodbyes. When we reached my place, Sade was knocked out, so I carried her into the house and laid her down in the guest bedroom. I took off her shoes and her jacket before tucking her in. The sounds of soulful old school music led me back downstairs. Raven stood next to my Christmas tree holding a medium sized box in fancy wrapping.

"I wanted to save the best gift for last," she spoke softly.

She handed me my present and I smirked then shook the box. Ripping at the wrapping paper revealed that she'd brought me a smart watch.

"Since you like to work out and run and stuff, I thought that you would like something like this. It has a heart rate monitor, a GPS, a timer, and syncs with your phone." She rambled on about all the specs while she unboxed it and placed it on my left wrist. Once it was secured on my wrist, I pulled her close.

"Thank you, Baby. It's perfect."

"You're welcome."

"There's something under that tree for a very special woman." Raven's eyes gleamed and she ran to the tree, locating the gift I had wrapped at the mall. She ripped the paper off and carefully opened the box.

"Diamonds!" she shouted. Then she gasped and was silent. In the box were a pair of diamond studs and a platinum and diamond necklace. The pendant hanging from the necklace was a sketch of her dad.

"Liam. This is... this is... I love it. Thank you so much." She jogged back to me and I wrapped her in my arms. Having this moment with Raven made my insides feel warm and whole. Being with her made me appreciate the small things. Raven slipped from my grasp and began to unbuckle my belt and pants. I raised an eyebrow. With a shake of my head, I pulled her back up. Raven held a look of dejection, but I quickly erased that when I kneeled to my knees and kissed her mound through her clothes. I inhaled her sweet arousal and groaned. My hands moved up her toned thighs then eased her underwear down.

"What are you doing, Mr. Washington? Ah shit, Baby."

"You just relax and let me properly wish you a Merry Christmas."

"Liam. Mr. Liam. Wake up."

Who is calling me? With one eye open I turned to the small voice. After a few blinks I realized that it was Sade. Her hair was all over her head and she was still wearing her clothes from the day before.

"Hey. Is everything okay?"

"Yes. Good morning. I'm hungry and Mommy won't wake up."

That's because I wore that ass out. The thought of all the nasty things Raven and I did to each other the night before made me grin.

"Yeah. Um, okay. Let Mommy sleep and I will make breakfast. Go take a shower and get dressed."

"Okay. Pancakes?"

"Pancakes it is."

"Yay!"

Sade skipped off to her room, unable to contain her excitement. I laid back down and watched the woman lying next to me sleep peacefully. Ray was a quiet sleeper, but she slept wild. Most nights when we slept together, she ended up with her leg draped across me or completely on top of me. I kissed her on the nose then climbed out of the bed. Once I washed up and tossed on some clothes, I completed a few sit ups and pushups then stretched before heading to the kitchen to get breakfast started. Sade was sitting at the counter waiting for me. By the sound of it she was talking to her dad. While they caught up, I busied myself with gathering everything I needed to make pancakes and sausage. After Sade hung up with her dad, she gave me her undivided attention. I let her help with mixing the batter and arranging a bowl of fruit. The sultry soulful music coming from up the stairs signaled that Raven had awakened. Ten minutes later she floated into the kitchen wearing dark gray joggers, a thin blue sweater, and matching fuzzy socks. She wrapped her arms around Sade then, kissed and tickled her. Sade's giggles filled the space.

"Good morning my beautiful honey bun."

"You're so silly, Mommy."

She sauntered over to me and hugged me from behind.

"Good morning. Did my baby wake you up to make breakfast?"

"What makes you think that?" I turned my head towards her.

"Because you are making pancakes when you are a protein shake or eggs and bacon type of guy."

"Well, she tried to wake up her mother, but she was laid out comatose." When I leaned back, she met me for a kiss.

"Oooo."

"Alright, little girl. Were you on your best behavior for Liam?"

"Yes, Ma'am, and I helped cook. Can I watch cartoons?"

"Sure. Just until breakfast is ready." Raven lovingly watched Sade skip to the couch and search for something to watch. She blushed when she caught me watching her. It was something that I couldn't help doing when we were in the same room together. Even when she was sleep, I found myself lost in her. She hopped on the counter next to me and popped a piece of mango into her mouth.

"Let me help."

"Alright. You want to cook up these pancakes while I fry up these sausages?"

"You're supposed to be making pancakes mister. How about I make the coffee, blend up some juice, and make the sausage."

"But I like the way you cook yours. All buttery with the crispy edged just the way I like them." I leaned into Raven and kissed her neck. My tongue swirled around her sensitive flesh before I made my way to her lips. With my free hand I pinched and tugged at her nipple.

"Mmm. You are lucky my child is here. You win. I'll make the pancakes. Yours still need work anyway."

We kissed a few more times before separating.

"Thanks, Ray. And you're the lucky one. Don't make me put that ass back to sleep." She rolled her eyes when I grabbed a handful of her ass.

The rest of the morning was dedicated to eating and watching Disney movies. The girls were snuggled up under blankets and I sat in the middle of the two. There was no denying how good this felt. I'd always thought that I would live my life as a man with no extra attachments besides the family I was born into. Now, I found myself thinking about what it would be like if I had a family of my own. The thought was daunting. What was more overwhelming was that when I envisioned my family it always included Raven and Sade, plus one or two. Although I didn't deserve them, my selfishness would not allow me to let them go. There was no way I could continue to hide who I really was. It was easy right now because we lived two hours away from each other, so Raven didn't get to witness me waking up from nightmares, the mood swings, the flashbacks, and the panic attacks. I'm definitely in a much better place than I was a few years ago but living with PTSD was a daily battle that I worked hard to manage. When Raven was around, I rarely had episodes. I knew I needed to have a conversation with her sooner or later, but I'd convinced myself that she would leave me once she got a glimpse of the ugly parts of me. Right now, I was going to enjoy these quality moments with her.

CHAPTER SEVENTEEN

Raven

We were all gathered for Sunday dinner at Rah's house. This Sunday was a fish fry and we dined on fried catfish, macaroni and cheese, greens, candied yams, and cornbread. I watched Liam from across the yard boding with Hakeem, Nelson, and Rayne's fiancé Darryl. We'd been off lately and had been having petty arguments. We never talked through our disagreements instead Liam would shut down and shut me out. Before we got to my sister's we argued because I was, once again, making us late. Rayne stood next to me and bumped my shoulder. I slowly sipped my red blend.

"Talk to me, Sis. You two are fucking up the Sunday vibes."

"I wish I knew Raynnie. He's just been so irritable lately. I've been walking on eggshells all weekend."

"That doesn't sound healthy, Ray. What are you going to do?"

"If I knew then we wouldn't be in this weird space. I'm going to get a shot of something stronger," I mumbled as I headed inside to where Hakeem hid his real liquor stash. After two shots of Brandy, I was already feeling better. Everyone was in the yard dancing except my tall, handsome, brooding man. I danced my way over to him and performed my sexiest moves. Reaching for the hand that was free from holding a beer I attempted to pull him up, but he shook his head. When I tried again some liquor spilled out of the glass he held. Liam jumped up and I stumbled back.

"Dammit, Ray, didn't I say no!"

"I- I- I'm sorry. I was trying to get you to relax." Rah handed me a napkin and I tried to help clean him up. Liam snatched it from me.

"I think you helped enough."

"Hey!" Rah yelled.

"Yo man it's not that big of a deal. It was a mistake. Chill." Hakeem stepped in between me and Liam and attempted to push him back. Liam growled then shoved him. Me and my sisters surrounded them to dissolve the situation.

"Woah! Hey! Liam." I moved around Hakeem and placed my hands on his chest.

"He didn't mean anything. He was looking out for me. I need you to calm down. The kids are watching. Everyone just back off. He's cool." The darkness in his eyes dissipated and he looked back at Sade.

"Baby, I'm sorry. Everyone I'm sorry. Do you mind if we go?"

"No, not at all. We can go back home to your place and relax."

"I'll be in the car." Without another word Liam walked away.

"What was that Ray? Is everything okay with Liam?"

"I don't know Sis, but hopefully I can get to the bottom of it."

"Why don't you and Sade stay the night with us? Give Liam time to calm down."

"I appreciate that Rah, but we will be fine. I love y'all. Goodnight."

The car ride home was quiet. Even Sade didn't make a sound. When we arrived at Liam's place, I quickly got Sade bathed and into bed. The mood was so off that I opted to shower alone. Just as I was rinsing off Liam slipped into the shower. As soon as our eyes locked his lips collided with mine and we got lost in a sloppy kiss. Liam lifted me around his waist and slipped inside of me as he pressed me against the wall. His deep strokes were anything but gentle, but he was hitting all the right spots. My nails scraped his back and I screamed through my orgasm. I rolled my hips as he continued to move in and out of me. Liam growled and bit down on my shoulder as he released inside of me. When he eased out of me, I winced and was already missing the feel of him.

"Raven, I'm sorry about this whole weekend. It had nothing to do with you."

"Why won't you talk to me about it?"

"You're not ready for all of that. I just need for you to trust me." Although I was hesitant, I nodded my head.

"Okay. Let's get some rest."

Liam bumping against me startled me awake. He was mumbling in his sleep and his furrowed brow along with the sheen of sweat on his body showed signs of distress. I was hesitant to wake him up, but I couldn't stand the look of torment on his face. Sitting up in the bed I gently shook him as to not startle him.

"Liam. Liam, baby, wake up." When I leaned over him and shook him again his hand shot up and gripped my neck so fast it took my breath away. He flipped me over and pinned me in between him and the mattress. I writhed under him and tried to scream his name, but Liam squeezed my neck harder. There was a dark, lethal, and distant look in his eyes. He was unrecognizable. Tears stung my eyes, and my body shook with fear. I mustered all the strength that I had and bucked against him. The move cause him to loosen his grip and I worked my fingers under his thumb and pulled it back.

"LIAM!" I yelled at the top of my lungs. He blinked, then his eyes widened before he released me and jumped back off the bed. I scrambled back into the headboard. I coughed and gasped for air. Liam looked as if he had no idea where he was until he looked at me again. *What the hell was going on?*

"Ra- Raven? Shit, Baby, I didn't mean to hurt you." He reached for me and I flinched. I couldn't hide that I was both shook and frightened.

"Ray don't do that. Come here. Please." Once I looked into his eyes and saw my Liam, I crawled towards him and fell into his strong embrace. When I felt Liam tremble, I held him tighter. I pulled back and held his face to force him to look at me.

"What was that?" Liam turned his head. He grabbed my wrists and pulled my hands down before he climbed out of the bed.

"Liam. Please don't shut me out," I pleaded. He shook his head and tried to brush it off.

"It was nothing. It was just a dream. Let's just go back to bed."

"You are crazy if you think I'm getting back in bed with you after you choked me."

"I didn't…"

"You choked me, Liam!" My voice cracked and more tears fell down my cheeks. "I thought that you were going to…" I couldn't finish my sentence. I couldn't form the words and the look of shame on his face halted my words.

"Know what? We don't have to talk about it. I'm sleeping in the guest room." When he didn't stop me, I was crushed. I snatched up my phone and slammed the door. Before climbing into the guest bed, I rinsed my face with cool water. A gasp escaped my mouth when I saw his handprints on my neck. There was no doubt in my mind that it would bruise. I rinsed away more tears before climbing in the bed and falling asleep. I woke up the next morning to a house that was eerily quiet. Liam wasn't a loud person but there was always some sort of background noise from the TV or radio. I quickly washed up and ran my fingers through my tapered cut. Liam wasn't in his room, so I made my way downstairs. Liam was sitting at the kitchen counter sipping coffee. He was shirtless and his basketball shorts sat low on his waist. He spoke with his back turned to me. The urge to wrap my arms around him was so strong. I followed the pull towards him then his words stopped me.

"This is not working for me, Ray." He didn't just say what I thought I heard. There was no way. No real reason.

"What? You can't be serious right now. *Liam.*"

"We are two different people. Neither one of us is what the

other person needs."

"What is this about? Is this because I was late for dinner with your dad? Last night?"

"It's about everything." The sound of his fist slamming into the counter made me jump. His shoulders slumped as he sighed.

"You're just going to break up with me and not even look at me. LOOK AT ME YOU FUCKING COWARD!"

Liam spun around with a scowl on his face that quickly morphed into horror and guilt when he saw the evidence of last night's scare on my neck. He stood up and took a step towards me then stopped. It was obvious by the look on his face that he was engaged in some sort of internal battle. My hands shot to my neck. I opened then closed my mouth.

"That right there is just another reason why we shouldn't do this anymore Raven." His tone was cold and void of emotion. It pissed me off.

"You know I knew you were a little type A-ish and a little guarded, but I never took you for an asshole. Fuck you, Liam."

I stormed back upstairs and quickly packed up my shit. I texted Rasheeda to tell her that I was on my way. Liam came upstairs and attempted to help me with my things, but I snapped at him. How could he be a jerk one minute then all chivalrous the next? I trudged to the guest room and scooped up my sleeping child. My chest tightened when I reached for the doorknob; I pulled my hand away. I turned around and there was Liam, standing behind me. I was tempted to drop my bags and show him all the reasons why I was the woman for him, but I needed him to drop his guard and make a move. Chasing Liam was getting old. I needed him to need me bad enough that he wouldn't dare allow me to walk out his door, but he made no attempts to speak or stop me. Maintaining my brave face, I placed my keys to his place on the table near the door and left.

"Is she dead?"

"Girl no she's not dead. What is wrong with you? Raven, Honey, get up! Rayne is here." I groaned and mumbled expletives before I rolled over and gave them my back.

"Hold on I got something for her ass. Rah, go open the curtains."

The curtains whooshed and I could feel the heat of the sun on my face. Cold water was doused on me and I shot straight up gasping for air.

"What the fuck?!" I shivered from the ice cold wake up alarm courtesy of my sister.

"That's what I want to know. Rah said that you've been locked up in her guest room for the last two days. What is going on with you? Did you forget that you have a child to care for along with her annoying ass baby daddy? He's been blowing up our phones because he can't reach you to see about Sade."

Hot tears filled my eyes and I fought like hell to keep them in. When Rasheeda disappeared into the adjourning bathroom, returned with a towel and wrapped it around me I could no longer hold it in, so I let them fall. I sniffed and angrily wiped my face.

"Liam broke up with me and I don't know why."

"Did he do that to your neck?" Rah spoke softly as she rubbed my arm. Her tone was sweet, but her energy was everything but that. I toyed with the option of lying but I'd promised to never lie to them again.

"Let me explain first."

"That's a yes or no question."

"Rah please..."

"Yes or no?!"

"Yes..."

"KEEM!" Rasheeda screamed.

"No! Stop. It wasn't like that. He didn't mean..."

"What Ray? He didn't mean to hit you. That is what all abused women say."

"He did not hit..."

The room door flung open and my brother-in-law Hakeem barreled in with his shot gun. I groaned and tried to massage away the headache that was forming.

"What's wrong?"

"Liam put his hands on Ray."

"No." No one was listening to me. They were all making plans on my behalf to defend me. Everything was spiraling too fast. I massaged my chest because my heart was pounding so fast.

"What the fuck? Where that nigga at?"

"Stop. Please. Just listen to me dammit!" The chaos settled and the room quieted. I appreciated my family's willingness to ride out for me, but they were wrong about this.

"Before you accuse and label him as something that he is not you need to shut up and hear me out. He was having a nightmare and I tried to wake him up and things just got out of hand, but he had no control. He was still sleep until I was finally able to wake him up. Liam would never purposefully put his hands on me." My family's' eyes were filled with worry. They wanted to call bullshit and do whatever they needed to do to protect me. Even if that meant Keem and his brother's finding Liam and beating his ass.

"I appreciate you all being so ride or die but you jumped to conclusions and your assumptions of what happened couldn't be farther from the truth."

"If what you say is true then maybe he did you a favor break-ing up with you, Sis."

"No. You just don't breakup after one crazy night."

"A crazy night that left you with bruises around your neck, Raven. There is obviously something going on with him. Maybe time apart is best."

I shook my head and hopped out of the bed. This wasn't how it was supposed to end. We weren't supposed to end. I thought he was the one. We were complete opposites, but I felt it.; the connection. I needed to see Liam and make him see that I could be what he needed. That I can help him. As if they could read my mind, my sisters blocked my path.

"You can't go back over to his house Ray. Give it time. Give him time." My eyes left Rah's and focused on Rayne's. She nodded her head.

"Please sissy. Plus, you look a mess." My eyes bucked and I

rushed to the mirror and at the horror looking back at me. I needed to brush my teeth, shower, and wash my hair. After that, I needed to spend time with my daughter.

"Where is Sade?"

"She's downstairs with her cousins painting. I told her that you were sick. Don't worry about her. Just get yourself together Ray. Don't fall back into old habits."

"Whatever *mother*." I mumbled under my breath. Brushing past my sisters I stepped into the bathroom and closed the door. After relieving myself, I turned the shower on and brushed my teeth while the bathroom filled with steam. The hot water felt so good that I moaned when it ran down my back. I was thankful that my sisters and I had similar tastes in body products. I lathered my skin with the Almond Cookie body wash and then washed my hair with the watermelon mint shampoo and conditioner. Outkast's *So Fresh, So Clean* flowed from my lips as I dried off with the plush towel. The shower did the trick. I was already feeling a little better, but the urge to reach out to Liam was still strong. With a shake of my head, I tried to push my pain back into the recess of my mind. I was a mother and a business owner. I needed to put on a brave face and push forward.

CHAPTER EIGHTEEN

Two Months Later

Liam

T he ballroom was dimly lit, so I maintained my place fitting in the background. I was dressed in my usual uniform, an all-black suit and tie. Tonight, I was hired to protect the daughter of a local congressman. Her father hinted at signing an annual contract with my company, but I wasn't so sure about that. Karmen Kane was a well-known socialite and was only famous because she went out and posted on social media. I didn't get that shit, but who was I to knock her hustle. Karmen was used to getting whatever she wanted and wasn't used to hearing the word no. In the two days that I'd known her she hadn't stopped flirting even with me remaining stone face and completely ignoring her. The Black Political Association was holding their annual charity fundraiser. This was my first year attending without Mr. G and it just felt off. Karmen strutted over to where I was trying to lay low. I rolled my eyes and didn't try to hide it.

"Am I bothering you, Mr. Washington? I thought that my father hired you as my bodyguard. How can you guard this body while standing way over here?"

"If you must know everyone in here has undergone an extensive background check courtesy of my team. We checked everyone in, and their image was scanned into our secured system.

There are also members of my team in this room right now, male and female. They blend in well don't you think?" Karmen tugged her bottom lip in her mouth and attempted to move in close. I stepped back and my eyes glared with warning.

"Oh, come on Mr. Washington. My father is working the room kissing ass. You don't have to be such a gentleman with me." When she didn't get a response there was a spark in her eye. She signaled a server over, not knowing it was a member of my team. She took a champagne flute off the tray and shooed her away. Bianca's lip curled up and then she winked at me before walking away."

"My dad and Gerald Jackson were good friends. They were frat brothers. Raven and I went to the same college, but she didn't fit in with the girls. It was like she loved being around the men whether they were spoken for or not. She had a bit of a reputation on campus. Most of us wasn't as *experienced* as she was."

I clenched my fist and bared down on my jaw so I wouldn't say something that was out of line. It was obvious that she knew that we dated or assumed that we still were. Raven wasn't shy about sharing our relationship with the world on her social media platforms. My eyes roamed the room.

"Ms. Kane if you don't mind, I would like to stay focus on what I was paid to do."

"And that was to *watch* me." She snapped and just that quick her mood brightened back up.

"It's apparent that you are not above dating your clients. I just want you to give me the chance to show just how much I can please you. There's no way Raven's a better option than me and she hasn't flaunted your relationship in a while, so I sense that there is trouble in paradise." Her hand ran up my chest and I could no longer take it. I grabbed her arm then dropped it.

"I am above it, but that was just how special Raven was; no *is*. You're nothing like her Karmen. Now please go and mingle like you came here to do and stop embarrassing yourself."

With a huff she turned around and stomped away. There was no way that I was taking on her or anyone in her family on as a client. This was a one and done situation.

It was three in the morning by the time I made it home. Karmen thought it would be fun to end her night at a party downtown. Securing the house, I tugged off my tie and grabbed a beer out of the fridge. My body sank into my sectional and I laid my head back. I was exhausted. Since ending things with Raven I'd thrown myself back into work putting in sometimes eighty hours a week and that was finally catching up with me. I refused to slow down because that would mean that thoughts of all the ways I messed shit up would flood my head or I would succumb to my PTSD. My therapist had left several voicemails and emails for me to check-in. I hadn't had a session in a month, and I knew that he was growing more concerned with time. Before I talked myself out if it, I grabbed my tablet and sent an email to my therapist suggesting a time for the upcoming week.

The sunlight shining through my huge window woke me up. My arm flew up and over my face as I attempted to block my eyes. I was still on the couch in my clothes from last night. My back was stiff and sore from the awkward position that I slept in.

"About time you woke your ass up. Get up and get this lunch."

"Nigga why you ain't wake me up?" I croaked.

"You usually wake up whenever I come in, but since you didn't even budge at my intrusion, I thought you needed the rest. You're not in the military anymore and you don't have to be up at the crack of dawn."

"You know it helps that I keep a routine."

"And it won't kill you to deviate from that sometimes. I know Raven and her chaotic ass ain't have no routine." I didn't respond. Instead, I went upstairs to shower and read my devotional before making my way back to my brother.

"You know you can't put up walls with me." This dude was like a dog with a bone. He can't let shit go. My head bobbed up and down.

"Look it was good while it lasted but shit ain't work out." I brushed past him and fixed me a plate of steak, mashed potatoes, and green beans.

"How's pops doing?"

"You know him. He ain't slowing down no time soon. He's worried about you."

"I told him I was fine."

"You say that, but we know you. I know you. I know the signs."

"Chill, man. I made an appointment with my therapist. I'm good."

I understood why he was worried about me. After I allowed Raven to close the door on us, I took a dive off the deep end. I'd took off from work and ignored everyone's calls. I'd even changed the code to my condo so no one could pop up. I was having more flashbacks and panic attacks, so it was just best for me to stay inside. Leith ended up breaking into my place and found me on my balcony drunk off my ass. The look on his face when he thought I wanted to jump ship sobered me up really quick. Since then, he checked on me every day. Either we talked, texted, or he popped up on me like today. We avoided talking about that night. Had dad known he probably would have tried to have me Baker Acted.

Leith fixed himself a plate and sat across from me at the table. We ate in silence for a minute. He was gaging my mood and temperament. I hated that he had to do that, but Leith sometimes knew me better than I knew myself. After eating enough to curve my hunger I sat back in my seat.

"I spazzed out on her. For I minute I didn't know who she was. I was dreaming about being in the war and I was in hand-to-hand combat. Next thing I know I blink then my hand was around her neck and I'm pinning her to the bed."

"Shit man."

"Exactly. I bruised her fucking neck with my handprints. It's the look in her eyes that haunt me. It was the same look she had the day of the attack. She was afraid of me man. She slept in the other room Leith. I knew then that I couldn't do this to her. She deserves better. Not running around finding ways to adapt to my PTSD and I know she would have. Raven would have been all in and I don't need her using her energy to fix me."

"Bro', you don't need fixing. I do think you need her energy though. She had a good effect on you."

"My ass needs to be regulated before I do anything. But I'm not fighting it. I'm getting my lady back. I just hope she gives me another chance."

CHAPTER NINETEEN

"**N**ow take a deep breath in. One, two, three, four, five. Now hold it. One, two, three, four, five, and release. Five, four, three, two, one. Let's do that two more times." Everyone sat on their individual mat sitting with their legs crossed with one hand on their stomach and the other hand on their chest. I started and ended all of my yoga sessions with breathing exercises. I closed it out with everyone lying in corpse pose. I slowly walked around the room speaking affirming words and spraying my blend of lavender and citrus oils in the air. The class laid peacefully on the floor and a few of my staff had joined. I instructed everyone that class was over, but they could get up whenever they felt ready.

"Raven this was one of your best classes. You've been in a zone all day today. It looks like that yoga retreat did you some good."

"More than you know." I smiled and winked at Yanika. We'd developed a friendship and had been hanging out whenever we had the time. After things ended with Liam, I found myself spiraling. I thought ignoring my pain would help, but it only made it worse. I could no longer hide from my grief by putting my energy into a relationship. I had to not only deal with a breakup but also my denial that I wasn't still grieving. It hit me hard too. I'm talking about putting my child to bed then drinking myself to sleep, not eating, ignoring calls from my sisters, and abandoning my responsibilities. When my shit started to trickle down to my child who was becoming more withdrawn each day, I knew I needed to get it together. I'd done some dumb crap in my life but had never allowed it to affect Sade and if her dad had gotten wind of what was going on, he would have done everything in his power to move her in with him. There was no doubt in my mind that I needed to get away, so I registered for this yoga retreat in Jamaica and it was exactly what I needed. The retreat was for women of color only. The energy was just amazing. I didn't leave Jamaica as the person I arrived as. We laugh, cried, healed, danced, smoked, encouraged each other, and bonded with each other over the course of two of the most amazing weeks. While away, I dealt with my pain and the bad decisions I made because of it. I dealt with the loss of my mother when I needed her the most. I dealt with the disappointment from my mistakes and the heartbreak from my affair with Tariq. I grieved the horrible loss of my father. Last, I grieved the loss of Liam and what I thought was my chance at real love. Yep, I fucked up and fell in love with the man. I never told him because I didn't want to scare him away, but that was just avoiding the inevitable. Hell, I still loved him, but it wasn't my job to get him to heal and open up to me. That was a choice he had to make. He couldn't do that while in a relationship. It was obvious that he's suffering through PTSD. I'd picked up on a few subtle symptoms, but the realization of my accuracy slapped me in the face that night he choked my ass while half awake. I was no longer angry with him and I forgave him for not trusting me with his pain. Jamaica was exactly what I needed. I came home healthy, whole, stronger, and with a clear mind.

"Are we still on for tonight?"

"Hell yes. I'm ready to shake my tight ass on somebody's son. My sister should be here already. She has keys to my place so she's probably home raiding my closet. I also invited Angie too since she's in town for work. Oh! I need to make sure Sade's sitter can still come over because I cannot have her ass flake on me tonight." I hated that I had to use my back up sitter. My normal girl had to study for exams, so I had to rely on the flake. What I needed to do was to get a better back up.

"Isn't Angie the chick that was trying to fuck your man?" Nika rolled her neck and frowned.

"Yes, but we've moved past that and I am single. Remember? I don't know why I told you that anyway. She's since apologized and she's actually good peoples. I like her." Angie and I had also grown closer. She was always calling to check on me and we would have some really great conversations. Overtime Angie had proven herself trustworthy. I finally decided to open myself up to her friendship and she's been a good friend since.

Music, food, boozy drinks, and my girlfriends was a new tradition that I now looked forward to and I was glad to finally include Angie. We were at a new spot that catered to the grown and sexy and I was feeling the vibes.

"Have you talked to him?"

"To whom?" I yelled over the music. Angie leaned back and gave me a look that said to stop bullshitting her. I knew exactly who she was talking about. I tossed back a lemon drop shot and danced in my seat.

"No, I haven't. I stopped chasing men when I broke things off with Tariq. I won't subject myself to that again. I'm not perfect but I was good to him and he just broke up with me and for what? Because he has PTSD and he's too afraid to share that with me." Angie's eyes widened in shock. She took a sip of her vodka tonic.

"Yeah, I know about the PTSD. I been picked up on it. My first degree is in psychology. How shallow does he think I am?"

"Ray, he doesn't think you're shallow. Fragile maybe, but not shallow. He respects you and thinks that you're the smartest thing on this earth."

"He talks about me?"

"Yes. Well, he used to. Now, he's crawled back into his shell and is even more of a recluse. Old grouch. He doesn't really talk to me anymore. You know I drove all the way to his house to check on him and he wouldn't let me in? The man is miserable without you."

Hearing that he was going through it just as much as I had made the corners of my mouth turn up, but it also made me worry about him.

"You wrong for thinking that's funny Ray." Angie scoffed and brushed her hair out of her face. She wore it bone straight with a part in the middle.

"The ball is in his court Angie. I love Liam so when he's ready I am here, but I won't put my life on hold for him. Maybe we are just too different and that will always come between us."

"Ugh. I can't with you two." She rolled her eyes and took a sip from her rum and coke.

"Are you two going to talk all night or get your asses up and dance with me and Nika?"

Rayne tugged my arm. I stood up and adjusted the white mini dress I was wearing. I pulled Angie and headed to the dance floor with Rayne and Nika. It was Vibez night at the club tonight, so they were playing a lot of Soca, Reggae, dancehall, and afro beats. The music created a sexy ambiance and me and my girls took over the dance floor winding and swaying our hips to the beat. I felt a presence behind me, and I was prepared to step out of their reach.

"You mind if I have this dance?"

"Allen?" I scrunched up my nose and turned around. It was my dad's advisor. Allen always dressed and looked so lame whenever he was around the estate. Tonight, he was dressed down in slacks and a button up. Nothing special but I could tell that he probably didn't have any problem attracting women. He was taller than average and had a nice smile. It was too slick looking for me, but it was still a nice smile.

"Hey! What are you doing here?" I didn't move when his hand went to my waist and he started moving with me.

"I have a job interview with a local company as a legal and political consultant."

"You're relocating here?"

"I'm thinking about relocating. I've applied to jobs in other cities as well."

"Oh, that's great. South Shores is a great city." I hadn't seen Allen since the public memorial service that was held for my dad once they caught his killers. He hadn't come over and spoke that day which I'd found to be odd, but we all grieve in our own way. Allen licked his lips and pulled me in closer. The liquor had me feeling good, so I went with the flow. We danced for a few songs before I stepped out of his hold.

"I better get back to my girls now. Take care Allen."

"Yeah, you too, Ray." He leaned in and placed a kiss on my cheek that lingered a little too long. I stepped back and nodded before seeking out my sister and friends. They were back at our booth munching on wings and fries. I sat down, popped a fry in my mouth and grabbed a wing.

"Ray was that Allen?"

"That was him."

"Dang. Either I am sexually deprived, or his ass was looking like a snack tonight."

"No, he was looking good. There's something different about him."

"What? Did he make you all wet, hot, and bothered?" Rayne wiggled her brows and shimmied.

"Eww Raynnie! Seriously."

"Uh huh. I saw how you were grinding on him."

"I second that." Nika chimed in and Angie nodded.

"You ain't have sex in how long? I wouldn't judge you if you wanted to see what old boy Allen was working with. You need maintenance. Let him be your service appointment. You haven't taken her for a spin in a while. You don't want that shit to stall up on you when you finally decide to put her to work."

"Are we talking about her coochie or a car?" Angie sputtered and we all cackled.

"Okay no more drinks for you two. I am officially cutting you ladies off."

"I'm okay with that. Come on, let's take this food to go and head back to Ray's. We smokin' tonight bitches."

The next morning, I woke up feeling like I was having an outer body experience. My mouth felt pasty and my head was spinning. I checked my phone and had missed calls and a text from Rasheeda. The text simply read "What the hell!!" I had no idea what she was talking about and was not in the mood to find out. I went to the bathroom and washed up. When I was met with the glorious smell of coffee, I knew it had to be Angie. Raynnie was sprawled out in my bed and I found Nika on the floor in my yoga room as I made my way down the hall and downstairs. Angie was sitting on the back deck holding a coffee mug. I made me a cup, added a shot of Rum Chata, and joined her.

"Hey girl. Anyone else up?"

"What do you think? After you tapped out, I was right behind you and those two stayed up so who knows what they were up to."

"Have you checked your social media?" Angie inquired with a smirk.

"No why?" I frowned then unlocked my phone and swiped to the app. That was where I discovered the videos and photos I'd posted. There were videos of us smoking, twerking, singing, and just having a good time. I laughed and covered my face. We all looked carefree and sexy, so I wasn't at all embarrassed. We had tons of likes and comments. I deleted anything that wasn't cute. I understood why Rah was mad, but this was nothing compared to the stunts Raynnie and I use to pull when we were in our twenties. Rah was all about protecting the family's image. I was fucking grown though.

"We look like baddies though."

"We do."

"Um. Liam finally called me." I paused my swiping and gave Angie my attention. My heart rate increased in anticipation.

"Yeah? What did he say? Did you two patch things up?"

"He told me that I better look out for you and if anything happens to you then that was my ass." Angie scoffed then smiled.

"That nigga hung up on me before I could respond back."

"Wow. Well, that's nice of him to still care." I rolled my eyes. My tone dripped with sarcasm.

"Call him Ray," Angie urged.

"No Angie. Hungry? I'm going to go pick up some breakfast."

"Need me to go with you?"

"Nope. Just get those other sleeping beauties up. They will not be laid up in my house sleeping all day."

I took to the boardwalk and walked to mine and Sade's favorite breakfast spot. The inside was designed like an old school diner and it was Black-owned. They had a vast menu which included vegan and gluten free options. I ordered a little bit of everything to accommodate everyone. After everyone was up and smelling fresh, we ate breakfast together then walked out to the beach to hang out. We had a good time relaxing, taking pictures, and playing in the water. I called and checked in on Sade and promised to pick her up in a couple of hours. She, Rayne, and I were having a movie night and Sade was excited. I went to my photo gallery and swipe through pictures of Liam. Most of them were selfies he allowed me to take of us. The others were some off-guard photos I took of him. Those were my favorites. I missed that man terribly. With a sigh I placed my phone on the towel and walked out to the water for a swim. The water was a little cold, but I didn't mind until I got out and was shivering. It had gotten cloudy and the wind was picking up. I jogged back to where the other ladies were sitting and chatting it up.

"You okay over there? You just popped up and ran to the water like your ass was on fire."

"Hush up Raynnie." I'm going to head in. I need to clean up and bathe so I can pick up my honey bun. We're going to the movie's tonight, so you ladies are more than welcome to join the three of us.

"Aww I would love to hang out with that beautiful genius, but I need to head back to Palm Lake today."

"Sorry, no can do. I promised one of the other managers that I would cover for them today so duty calls," Nika responded. We all gathered our belongings and closed out what was an epic ladies night out.

Sade, Rayne and I ended up loading up on snacks and going to the drive-in. They were playing *A Wrinkle in Time*. It was a book I read to Sade and it was now one of her favorite movies. I backed my Jeep in and popped the trunk open. The back was laid out with pillows and blankets. This was what being a mom was all about. Quality time with my little girl. Having her snuggled up under my side warmed my heart. If no one else ever loved me my little rider would; unconditionally.

I checked my phone and had another missed call from my father's attorney. I'd skipped out on the reading of his will and there were some papers I needed to sign. My sisters were given a generous sum of money, but my father pretty much left me with everything, and it was overwhelming. With my inheritance I could do whatever I wanted; I didn't have to worry about money ever again. There were so many decisions that needed to be made, specifically about the house. I didn't want to sell it, but I couldn't muster the courage to return. The thought of being there made my chest hurt; it was terrifying. I continued to pay his staff and hired a property manager to maintain the estate. Rasheeda and Hakeem stopped in periodically. They were each god sends. Eventually, I needed to put on my big girl panties and take care of business, but I honestly wasn't ready. As a thirty-five-year-old woman I still needed my parents and I no longer had them. The feeling of loneliness took over and I knew I couldn't succumb to the emotions of sadness and despair that came with that. I swiped at my nose with a back of my hand before I reached for my phone.

"Hey, Ray Ray boo."

The adoration and affection in her voice already had me feeling better. I produced a half laugh then broke down.

"Raven... Honey it's okay. Talk to me."

"I just miss them so much Rah. This shit hurts me to my core. To not have either of my parents... What did I do to deserve that?"

"This is not your fault. It's not some type of punishment for things you've done wrong. As messed up as it sounds, that's life. The good thing about it is that you have us, your sisters, Sade, my dad, Liam..."

"I *don't* have Liam, remember?" I scoffed then rolled my eyes.

"You do. Believe me. You don't have to see him to have him. If you called that man right now, he would come running. It may not be apparent to you, but we see the influence you have over Liam. He may be working through his own demons but believe me, everything he does is with your best interest and protection in mind."

"Tuh. You sound like you're talking from experience."

"I am. Keem and I had some bumps in the road before we got to where we are. He came with baggage. Baggage that he tried to protect me from. When I pushed and he finally told me, I couldn't handle it and that crushed him. You remember when we broke up after a year of dating?"

"How could I forget? You were such a bitch."

"I was a hurt bitch, and I don't want you to make the mistakes that I made. I get the feeling that Liam would not be able to handle you rejecting him. When he shares whatever it is that made him push you away be prepared to take that shit like a G."

"Take that shit like a G huh? Who are you and where is my oldest sister?"

"Girl please. Don't forget I taught you and Raynnie everything I know."

"Yeah, then got married and went Mother Theresa on us." I joked.

"Whatever. It's okay to be sad and cry Ray."

"I know. It just consumes me sometimes and that terrifies me."

We sat on the phone silently enjoying the company. I sat on my bed organizing pictures for Self-Love when an idea hit me. My eyes sparkled with excitement.

"Rah what do you think about me turning the estate to a bed

and breakfast? Not your typical b-n-b but include a wellness component, a wellness retreat aspect. The estate already has the lake, a pool, jacuzzi, the garden, and a tennis court. There would be a spa, yoga and meditation classes, and—"

"It's a brilliant idea Ray!" Rasheeda gushed over the phone.

"Really!? You really mean that?"

"Yes, and if you don't mind, I would like to help, and we can pull Raynnie in and make it a sister thing."

"Hmm. Sisters Three B and B or Radiant House."

"I like Radiant House." With a smile on my face, I nervously bit my nails. Thinking of the possibilities and if I could truly pull this off.

"Only when you're ready, Sis." I smiled because my big sis knew me well. Even when it got on my nerves sometimes. I couldn't ask for a better sister. Rasheeda filled the motherly role that I needed.

"Thanks, Rah. I love you."

"I love you too, Ray Ray."

CHAPTER TWENTY

Liam

The room buzzed with chatter and music to set the mood. Holding a glass of cognac, I walked around the room and studied each piece of art. Each pulled at a different emotion. I stood in front of a painting that had captured my attention more than the others. My head tilted to the side as my eyes moved over the work of art. It was abstract but obvious that it was the face of a woman looking towards light. The lips curved like she knew something you didn't know, and her eyes held a familiar glint of mischief.

"Like what you see?" Leith bumped my shoulder. An arrogant look of satisfaction was on his face.

"She knows you got her face plastered on this canvas?"

"Sort of. Yes. Just not that it's a part of my exhibit. I'd never done this style before and needed a little practice. She helped me out. I painted this while we were at Angie's." I shook my head and took a sip of my drink.

"It's amazing man. Congratulations on tonight."

"Thanks, Bro'. Well, you enjoy. I'm going to finish finessing these folks out of their money." We pounded fists before he moved towards a group of women who were fawning over a sketch of a man wearing barely anything. It was him or me... *This motherfucker.* When he caught me looking, he pointed in my direction and I became the second object of the group of women's desires. Goosebumps prickled up my arm. My instincts put me on alert. I turned towards the door and watched Raven strut in with her sisters. She was wearing black cut up jeans over a black body suit, and a colorful sequins kimono. The black heels made her taller. Her eyes met mine and my heart skipped a beat, but she quickly turned her head and walked in the opposite direction. I accepted the rejection for now because I had no doubt that she was leaving with me tonight.

I walked around the space watching Raven work her way through the exhibit. She laughed with her sisters and strangers. People were drawn to her just like I was. Whenever she moved, I found myself moving. I watched as she looked at the pieces with curiosity or amusement. When she landed in front of the one of her, her hands went to her mouth and she looked around for Leith who joined her. She looped her arm around his and looked like she was singing his praises.

"Are you going to talk to her or stalk my sister all night? Didn't take you as a scary cat."

"Careful, not scary. Don't worry. She'll be spending the night at my place."

"Oh. Okay there's that big... um, energy I heard about." I stared at Rayne quizzically. She waved as she headed over to the bar. I notice Leith's gaze following her after she sauntered past him. *What the hell is up with those two?*

Not wanting to waste another moment I ambled towards Raven. Her back was turned as she was occupied with studying a painting. When I approached her from behind, I inhaled her addictive scent. My hands landed on her shoulders then I moved them down her arms. The simple touch made her gasp.

"We need to talk." My lips brushed against her ear. I held my hand out and she placed her delicate hand in mine. I led her out back where there was a patio area to hang out. We stood far off in a corner. Raven pulled her hand from my grasp and crossed her arms in front of her chest. She looked stronger. When her father was killed, she held a look of uncertainty in her eyes every now and then. That was now gone. She waited for me to speak. When her eyebrows raised, and she moved her head from side to side I smiled.

"Baby I want to apologize for what I did. For ending things the way that I did. Shit, for ending things period. It was childish and cowardly. There are things that I was afraid to tell you and parts of me that I wanted to protect you from it."

"I'm a big girl, Liam. You don't have to protect me."

"Yes, I do." I gritted. "I love you, Raven, and I would give my life for you. I love that you are so outgoing and generous. I love how you love others. I love that you are fearless and sexy as hell. You're not afraid to show off your intelligence and you're un-apologetically you. You are everything to me."

"You love me?" She stammered over her words.

"Yes." I smirked then kissed her hands. "There are things that I need to tell you, but not here."

"Um, okay. Your place?"

"Yeah. Let's go."

"Wait. I can't leave without telling my sisters..."

"Text them in the car, Raven."

"Okay. Let's go."

It was quiet in the car on the way to my condo. I was pretty sure we were both in our heads. I was in my head playing over how this conversation was going to go, best case and worst-case scenario. After I let us in and secured the place, we got comfortable outside on my balcony overlooking the city. Raven curled up on the lounger next to me and wrapped herself up in a blanket.

"You have PTSD, Liam," Raven declared.

"What? You- you know?"

"All the signs were there, and you forgot that I am a smart girl." She tapped the side of her head then winked at me.

"That you are, but it's not just that. My nightmares are violent. You experienced it first-hand. Also, I suffer from flashbacks which causes panic attacks. It doesn't happen often, but when it does it's like I have no control over it. The only thing I can do is work through it. When it comes..." I shook my head and rubbed my palms up and down my thighs. Raven sat up and clutched my hand. The warmth of her small hands and the look of encouragement gave me the assurance I needed to continue. "It's terrifying not to be in control. Not knowing if some smell, loud sound or someone will set me off." I paused and studied her eyes. I needed to see if anything had changed. When she nodded her head, I felt okay to continue.

"I have violent tendencies, Ray. I've done shit that... I've done some fucked up shit. Being in the marines saved me but it also fed it. I lived for combat in the beginning especially hand to hand combat. It used to give me a rush, like a drug. Eventually, I found myself looking in the mirror and not recognizing the person staring back at me. That day when Gerald was killed, I regressed back to my old ways and killed two of those men with my bare hands Ray and a part of me enjoyed it. That shit felt good. Even though I'm not the person I use to be these things are still part of me. Can you..."

"Yes." She climbed on my lap and wrapped her arms around me.

"Raven you didn't let me finish."

"If you were going to ask me if I can love you knowing what I know then the answer is yes Liam. Do I view you differently knowing the truth? No, I don't. True love is unconditional Liam. Can you accept my love and know that you deserve it? That there is nothing you can do for me to take my love away?"

"I'll do anything to keep you and to make you happy." Raven's hand caressed the side of my face. She leaned in and her soft lips lightly touched mine before she finally kissed me. I wanted her to make the first move. I held her tighter as we made out on the balcony. She whined when our lips separated.

"Can I taste you now?" Raven laughed out loud and snorted. She tried to cover her mouth and I pulled her hands down. She looked at me lovingly.

"Took you long enough."

"Liam, I need a break. Please. Ah… mmm." Liam entered me for the umpteenth time. He gave me reprieve and allowed me to rest, but after only a few hours of sleep I woke up on the cusp of another mind-blowing orgasm; prepping me for another round. He was insatiable. Liam eased into my wetness and grunted. He sucked the side of my neck then began to move inside of me with precision and purpose. My yoni adjusted to him and then liquified as he angled himself to get me to my peak quickly. I clenched my muscles to hug him tight. That move would have him coming right along with me. Liam kissed my neck then found my mouth and our tongues tangled and explored. His groans and my panting filled the room as we both climbed higher and higher. Our eyes locked and the love and affection that was in this man's eyes cause me to lose it.

"Oh! Yes! Yes!" My pelvis bulked forward, and Liam held me tight as he groaned then released inside me. He fell on top of me, but I didn't mind his weight on me. It was actually soothing for me; to be chest to chest with him. Eventually he rolled over and laid on his back; he interlocked his hands with mine. My heart swelled.

"Baby that's it. I am officially tapping out. You've wore the kitty out. She's tired."

Liam pulled me in the spoon position and chuckled, sending vibrations through my chest. He wrapped me safely in his arms and hummed a familiar Maxwell song lulling me back into a peaceful sleep.

It was after twelve in the afternoon, by the time I woke up. I was alone in the bed. There was a note on the nightstand from Liam letting me know that he had to drop by his office and would be back around one. After reading the note I hopped out the bed and quickly washed up so I could prepare something for us to eat or I would be sitting across from him drinking a disgusting protein shake. By the time he arrived I was finishing up breakfast tacos and making fresh juice with pineapples, apples, oranges, and ginger.

"It smells good in here." Liam wrapped his arms around me and pressed into me. His arousal was unmistakable. I moved away from him and giggled.

"No! We are going to enjoy brunch and slowly settle into things again."

"After what we did last night, I think we are way passed moving slow." He smacked me on my ass, and I squealed. His only response was to smirk and wash his hands at the sink. We fixed our plates and took our food and drinks outside. I scarfed down my food as he looked on in amusement.

"What?"

"Nothing. I like that you don't hide yourself from me. You have no problem being who you are."

"It drove my parents crazy, but they instilled it in me. You either take me or leave me." I shrugged and took a huge bite of my taco and moaned.

"So good. Sade is going to be so excited to see you. She'd been asking about you and to be honest I didn't know what to tell her."

"That's what's up. I miss her too. How's she doing with her guitar?"

"She is doing amazing! She's even writing her own songs. Be prepared because she is going to want to play for you."

"I look forward to it."

"You know, she's never taken to anyone as quickly as she's taken to you. Sade is usually very careful about letting strangers in, but she wasn't like that with you. For some reason your mean ass made her feel comfortable."

"I'm good with kids." I nodded in agreement.

"That you are... but my baby saw something in you." I watched Liam as he finished off his food then took in the scenery outside. Everything was so damn sexy about this man from his dreamy eyes, to his chiseled jaw, kissable lips, and perfect teeth.

"Ray. Stop." He chuckled.

"What? Do you know how fine you are?" Liam blushed and

shook his head. I sat back in my chair and rubbed my full belly.

"All jokes aside, how are you doing?"

"Better. I've been seeing my therapist and taking my meds consistently. One of the things that came up in a session was how much I work. I was doing too much and dealing with the death of your dad had a greater effect on me than I was willing to admit. To address that I've stopped personally providing protection service. I hired more people and I'm only dealing with the business and training side of it all. There was only one thing that was missing."

"And what was that?"

"You." He leaned over and his lips softly pressed into mine. Liam's kisses were so sensual and salacious. Kissing him made me blush like I was doing some dirty shit. He always left me needing more.

"You talked to your therapist about me?"

"We did talk about you and he wanted to curse me out for pushing such an amazing person away. I came to realize that I wasn't going to ruin or taint you."

"Although how you ended things hurt me to my core, I believe that it was necessary. I am an all or nothing type of person and I would have lost myself in trying to fix you and mend us. I would have tried to fix you and I realized that whatever you were going through you needed to work through it yourself. We needed to come to each other whole."

"You were the light that I needed Ray."

"I know and you were the rock, the stability that I needed."

"I think your father knew."

"Knew what?"

"That we would be here. He knew if we just met, we would hit it off. When he hired me, I wasn't working the clients hands on anymore, but he insisted. Then that weekend of his birthday he kept looking at me like he knew something I didn't and pulled me aside to talk about me settling down. He would hint at you."

"Really?" My eyes widened. They were glossed over but I smiled.

"Yeah. Guess he knew I was a good catch."

"Boy whatever!" I punched him in the arm then giggled. Liam cleared his throat.

"So, what's really up with you and Angie?"

"Oh, she didn't tell you? We're besties now. She might even like me better than you since you put your girl on ice."

"You need her more than I do so I'm cool with that."

"Liam! That was mean."

"It's the truth. I'm not holding what she did against her..."

"Seems like it."

"Can I finish?" His expression was serious, so I nodded.

"I can't move past what she did. It may have been a lapse in judgment, but Angie knows me, and she knew that for me to be with you the way I was that there had to be feelings. Instead of talking to me about her feelings she tried to jump my bones while you were in the same house. I can't rock with that. You and Angie needed a friend so I ain't mad that you two have grown closer. We cool, but it won't ever be the same." He stood up and cleared the table. I followed him into the kitchen and sat at the counter. He statement had me thinking.

"Do you think I'm naïve for being friends with her?"

"Nah. That shit she did was sneaky, but she's not a liar or a malicious person. She really likes you and you mentioned not having many female friends."

My phone rang and I searched the living room until I found it in between the sectional cushion. Allen's name flashed on the screen and I sent the call to voicemail. He'd found a job in South Shores and I did some apartment hunting with him. I could tell that he was seriously feeling me, so I had to pump the breaks on him. At the time I was craving male company, but it wasn't fair to lead him on.

"Who was it?" Liam asked protectively after witnessing me ignoring the call. I chewed my bottom lip and massaged the back of my neck.

"Um, it was Allen."

"Allen? What the fuck are you...?" Liam bit his bottom lip

then released a rush of air. "Yo, my bad."

"What has Allen ever done to you Liam?"

"He gives me snake like vibes. I don't like him, and I don't like the way he looks at you. Why was he calling you?"

"You don't have room to question me Liam."

"I disagree. Tell me." We stood from across each other at a standoff. I crossed my arms and gave all the attitude that I could muster.

"Raven. I do not have time for games."

"Ugh! You can be such a brut sometimes. We ran into each other at a club. He has a new job in South Shores, and I have been helping him with apartment hunting."

"Well, you can dead that." I approached Liam ready to argue against his request but decided against it since I'd already decided to distance myself from Allen.

"Okay, fine."

"Look, I'm not doing this to control you and it's not out of jealousy. I need you to trust me when I say that I don't trust him and his motives." His eyes held genuine concern.

"I trust you. I'll let him know that we're together and it's best that we don't talk."

"Thank you. Here." He handed me a shopping bag. Bouncing with excitement I looked inside to find work out clothes and a very specific type of shoe. Shit.

"Babe. Where are we going?"

"We're going on a hike bourgeois princess." He kissed me on the lips then headed towards his room.

"Liam!"

CHAPTER TWENTY-ONE

Liam

W e stood in the middle of the living room floor. All of the furniture had been pushed around the perimeter of the room to give us space to practice. Sade stared at me intently as I got down to eye level. Her expression was as serious as mine was.

"Okay so we are going to practice what you would do if you were ever grabbed by someone who wanted to hurt you. Are you ready?"

"Yes, Sir," she answered in a hush tone.

"Alright. Let's go."

I stood up straight and stalked around Sade. Her chest heaved up and down. Without warning I grabbed her in a bear hug from behind and lifted her off the floor. The front door flung open and hurricane Raven came tumbling in.

"I'm so sorry…"

"Head butt!" As she was taught, Sade flung her head back with all the force she could muster and made contact with my face. I move my head just in time to miss the next two head butts.

"Ah shit! Baby Girl, wait." When her feet landed on the floor Sade turned around. Her eyes darted to her mother and back to me.

"I'm sorry. I didn't mean to," she whimpered. Her bottom lip trembled just like her mom's. I kneeled in front of her and wiped her tears.

"Hey. Don't do that. You did good, okay? You did exactly what I taught you. I'm fine."

"Are you teaching my child self-defense?" Raven dropped her bags. Her tone was serious and similar to that of your favorite Black TV mom. Both Sade and I whipped our heads back in her direction.

"Of course. I taught you so I thought she could benefit from learning some techniques."

"Liam."

"What?"

"She is a child. Honey go upstairs and wash up while I work on dinner." She kissed her then shooed her off.

"Kids get attacked and kidnap every day." Her expression was deadpan.

"What?!" I shrugged then began putting the room back to its original state.

"Are you trying to give me anxiety? You are showing your crazy and I need you to relax. I do not want you turning my child in to some killing machine."

"Like me?" Her sarcastic smirk faded.

"What? Liam no." Raven sauntered over to me and wrapped her arms around my waist. I met her halfway for a kiss.

"I appreciate you wanting to make sure that my child is protected. Just give me a heads up and remember she's a child."

"We played Jenga too."

"Balance. I like that. Are you okay?" Raven stood on her toes and pulled my face closer as she examined me.

"Yeah. She's strong as hell. For a minute there I thought she broke my nose." Raven kissed my nose several times. My hands massaged her back then worked their way down to her ass. I pulled her closer to me.

"Thank you for picking her up for me. Today was a crazy day.

We blew a fuse and… it was a mess. Just give me thirty minutes and I will have dinner ready. I promise." Raven headed for the kitchen, but I grabbed her and pulled her back.

"Now it's my turn to tell you to relax. It's okay. We can order pizza."

"Are you sure?" Raven was doing it again. Since we got back together, she had this little Miss perfect act she put on whenever we were together. She would break her back to make me comfortable like I would snap at any moment. I had yet to bring it up because I thought that it was her adjusting to us getting back together. But here she was again, trying to cater to me. I didn't need that.

"Yes. The Raven that I know would have ran up in here with a couple of pizzas. You don't have to always be on it when you're around me. Just be you. The woman that I love. The woman that I fell for."

"I am trippin' ain't I? Pizza it is."

"I'll order it."

"Okay! I'll go shower. Order the wings too. With blue cheese! Love you!" she yelled as she ran upstairs.

The three of us camped out on the living room floor eating and watching TV. Sade gave us a run-down of her day and soon she was sprawled out on the floor sleep. Raven and I sat with our backs against the couch. She sipped from her glass of wine and hummed. My arm was draped across her shoulders and my fingers made circles around her arm. There was a knock on her door. She made a move to get up, but I placed my hand on her thigh. It was late and anyone she knew would have called. Raven rolled her eyes and groaned with I lifted my gun from my bag. I looked through the peephole then cursed before I flung the door open.

"It's late Allen." He looked like a deer in headlights. It was almost comical. A man like him was only showing up at Raven's house at this time of night for only one thing. The thought made me want to dismember him.

"Liam. What are you doing here?" He glared at me like I was

imposing on his territory, but he was on mine.

"My presence was requested. What's your reason? Like I said. It's late."

"Is Raven here?"

"Allen? Is everything okay?" I turned and gave Raven a look that had her stepping back. "Yeah. You handle that. I'm going to put Sade to bed." I heard her mumble "old brut" as she walked away. My tongue traced my bottom lip and I fought back a smile.

"You've seen Raven so now you can go, but don't come back here."

"What do you mean? Look man you have no say in who she spends her time with."

"The hell I don't! Stay the hell away from her. I know she told you what was up, but here you are trying to force your way in. Don't let me catch you here again." I let the door slam in his face. My hands were itching to kill. I sat downstairs doing deep breathing exercises until I was calm and no longer had the need to confront Raven. I wanted to know why he knew where she lived and why he was so comfortable showing up at almost twelve in the morning. Raven stood in front of me. She ran her hand over the top of my head. I gripped her thighs and rested my head on her stomach.

"Please come to bed." I kissed both of her thighs then looked up at her. When she held her hand out, I grabbed it and stood up. I allowed her to lead me back up the stairs and into her room. I took a quick shower then went to check on Sade and made sure that the house was secured before I joined her in the bed. While in the bathroom I sent a message to Glitch to ask him to do a deeper dive into Allen and to include his family. The initial search came up short but there were gaps in his history that concerned me. I pulled Raven closer to me and got comfortable. Her sweet earthy scent relaxed me. The thought of anything happening to her and Sade not only made my blood boil, but it scared the shit out of me.

"Babe, are you okay? Your heart is pounding." She tried to turn to face me, but I held her tighter then placed a soft kiss on the back of her neck.

    "Stay away from him Ray."

    "O- okay."

CHAPTER TWENTY-TWO

Raven

Although I didn't understand Liam's beef with Allen, I decided to trust him and respect his wishes. My relationship with Liam meant more to me than being acquaintances with Allen. I still felt bad because he was new in town and I was the only person he knew besides the people he worked with, but I kept my word to Liam. I ignored his attempts to reach out to me and, eventually, he stopped. Things had been going great with Liam and me. It was a little bumpy in the beginning, but we were committed to our love. I was in love again and it was so much better than the first time. Our love was honest, unconditional, and healthy. We were at a great place right now and I'd been thinking about moving back to Highland City and renting out my home here in South Shores. My sisters and I were in the process of renovating the estate in preparation of the grand opening of Radiant House Bed and Breakfast Retreat. At this point the majority of what was important to me was back home in Highland City. When I brought it up to Liam, he told me that he would support whatever decision I made, but I caught the smile that he failed at hiding. He wanted me close and I didn't like going days without seeing or touching him. Like right now.

He was moving around the room packing up his bag while Sade and I sat on the bed pouting. We hated this part of the visits. It felt like we were living separate lives in separate worlds and I didn't like it. My phone alerted me that a Facetime call was coming through and I slid it over to Sade.

"Hey daddy." She spoke somberly. It was cute how close she and Liam had gotten. He was so gentle and patient with her.

"What's up baby girl. Hey, what's wrong?"

"Mr. Liam is leaving."

"This nigga..." Tariq groaned.

"Hey! You better watch your mouth," I chided.

"What up Ray. Liam?"

"Yeah, what's up?"

"Ain't shit man. You staying sane over there?"

"You know it. Nothing I can't handle." I tossed a pillow at Liam who blocked it with his arm.

"All jokes aside, I wanted to say thank you for pouring into my baby girl. She showed me the moves you taught her. She almost took me out with them but thank you."

"It's no problem at all. You and Ray raised an amazing little prodigy. I care about her as if she was my own."

"I wish I could take even half of the credit for Sade but that's all Raven."

"Is that a compliment from my baby daddy?" I was genuinely surprised. Even though we got along for the most part we had underlying issues that we always tap danced over.

"Yes Ray. I don't say it much, but I lucked up to have you as my baby mama."

"We've come a long way. Thank you."

"Daddy can you and I talk now?" Sade huffed. She hopped off the bed and ran out of the room. Like me, she didn't like sharing her daddy.

"That was good. Right?" I grinned from ear to ear.

"Yeah, it was. He's still in love with you." There was no way I would deny what was obvious.

"He is, but I am hoping now he puts his energy into being the husband his wife deserves. There was no way he could do that still thinking I was fair game. I won't lie. I fed into that by still carrying on a sexual relationship with him even after Sade was born. Thankfully I met the most amazing, sexiest, mean ass man that I had to have all to myself." Liam grinned, gracing me with that panty wetting smile of his and I knew I needed one last fix before he hit the road. He zipped up his bag and approached me. I was still sitting so I reached for his belt and pulled at the strap. The anticipation of tasting him made me salivate. I licked my bottom lip and tugged his pants down.

"Raven…"

"We will be quick and quiet. She will be on the phone with her bestie for at least an hour."

"We should still lock the door and it's never quick and quiet when it comes to you." Liam took a step back and went to close then lock the door. I followed so when he turned around, I dropped to my knees and gave my love a proper farewell.

"Like I said. Never quick and quiet."

"Mmm I'm sorry. It's just that…"

"You're spoiled?"

"I'm in love with your ass." Liam rolled on top of me and planted feather soft kiss all around my upper half. I giggled and squirmed under him. "Liam stop! Please!"

"Alright. I need to get out of here anyway. I told my dad that I would stop by before I went home." Liam gripped my hips and teased my nipple with his tongue before climbing out of the bed. I was already missing his warmth.

"Get up Raven." Liam tossed me my clothes and I got dressed. Neither of us had showered or washed off. I wanted the smell of us to linger. Once we were both dressed, I followed him downstairs. Sade didn't like goodbyes, so she always hid when it was Liam's time to leave. Stopping at the door Liam gave me a quick kiss on the lips.

"You lock up. Tell Sade I will see her in a few days."

"Okay and you better call me when you get in."

"I love you Raven."

"I love you too." We kissed one last time before he headed for his car. I hung outside by the door and watched him hop in his truck and back out of the driveway. He flashed his lights signaling for me to go inside. I blew a kiss. I closed the door and locked it. Sade came downstairs with her head hung low and her lips poking out. She took one slow step at a time. When she approached me, she wrapped her arms around me.

"Liam told me to tell you goodbye and that he would see us in a few days." I kissed her forehead. I'd washed her hair earlier, so they were in six long braids.

"Why can't he stay? Why can't you be like auntie Rah and uncle Keem?"

"Well, your auntie and uncle are married."

"So then get married." Sade looked at me like I missed the mark on something so simple.

"It's not that simple, Honey Bun, and I don't want you to worry about that. Let's eat dinner so you can get ready for bed. You have school tomorrow and I need to drop you off early so you'll eat breakfast there."

Sade was tucked in bed and I was looking forward to curling up on the couch with a cup of tea and a good book. With my latest romance novel tucked under my arm I jogged downstairs. The male figure standing in my living room stopped me in my tracks and I dropped my book. My eyes darted around the room.

"Allen. How did you get in here?"

"The door was open, and I was worried."

"But how..." There was no way the door was open. I clearly remember locking it. Allen's eyes darted around the room and moved around me like he couldn't stand still. His energy was off, and my defenses kicked in. When he stepped closer to me, I took a step back.

"Don't do that. You've been ignoring my calls and you've been hanging out with Liam again. That man has violent tendencies, and I was worried. I've always worried about you and I'm always looking out for you. Even when you don't know it. I want you to have the best of everything and I will do whatever it takes to en-sure that happens." His tone was eerily calm.

My gut was telling me something was not right. There were all types of alarms going off in my head. Sade was upstairs in her room and I prayed that she'd already fallen asleep. Allen walked to the front door and locked it.

"Um, I have plans. Can we do this another night?" In an in-stant his face morphed into a scowl.

"Plans with who, Liam? He fucks you and toss you aside and you just run back to him. He doesn't love you like I do. *He* hasn't sacrificed like I have. Everything I have done has been for you. I risked it all. While I was handling things with the senator you were fawning all over him. I wanted you to have everything that was owed to you, Raven. Your dad was stopping you from getting your inheritance and I took care of it for you." My head snapped up and my eyes narrowed. His mouth creeped up to a menacing smirk.

"What did you just say?" My parents set up a trust fund for me before I took my first breath and since then it had accrued a substantial amount of money. I was supposed to get it after I graduated from college, but after a few bad decisions, my father decided to hold on to it.

"What did you do?"

"He was always going to hold your trust fund over your head to control you, Raven."

"So, you had my father killed? You sick bastard!" I rushed Allen and slapped the shit out of him. "You could *never* have me. You're not man enough for me and Daddy would have never ap-proved of you." I looked him up and down. Disgust was written all over my face.

"Shut up!" Allen hauled off and backhanded me. I stumbled back before falling onto the floor. He tried to approach me, and I scooted back. "Dammit you ungrateful bitch! Look what you made me do! That's always been your problem. You got too much damn mouth! I'm trying to give you the world Raven. Come here sweetheart. Let me help you up."

"Don't touch me! You're crazy." I fought as he gripped me by the front of my shirt and yanked me on my feet. He was stronger than I thought. Once he had me on my feet, he pulled out a gun and pointed it around.

"Anyone else here Ray?"

"N- N- No." I prayed that Sade was already fast asleep and that he didn't try to go upstairs. I did my best to keep my eyes focused on him and not towards were my daughter laid her head. My phone's ringtone blasted, and I jumped from my nerves being shot. I knew it was Liam based on the song. I headed for my phone and Allen side-stepped me. He shook his head and made a sound by tapping his tongue into his teeth.

"Can I get a few minutes of your undivided attention? IS THAT SO FUCKING HARD!" His voiced boom throughout the house and I just knew Sade had woken up. I just hoped she remembered what I taught her. Because I was a single mom, and it was just the two of us, we had a plan in place for situations like this. Sade's role was to hide in this little hidden door that was in her closet and not to move until I came and got her. My phone rang again, and I hoped like hell that it would alert Liam to turn back. The pitter patter of little feet caused both of us to look up. He looked back at me and smiled.

"Is that Sade?"

"You stay the fuck away from her." A struggle ensued as I fought to keep him from going up the stairs. He attempted to push me, so I jumped on his back and clawed at his face. We ended up in the living room where he got me off his back and flung me into the coffee table. I gritted my teeth and held my side in pain.

"See! I knew you liked it rough." Allen waved his finger at me. He kneeled onto the floor and yanked me into him by my legs. My maxi dress was pushed up my thighs as I kicked and screamed. I panicked when I heard the distinct sound of him removing his belt and unzipping his pants.

"Allen, please don't do this," I pleaded.

"Don't worry. I'll give you exactly what you deserve. Fucking slut. You still smell like him." I bucked my body when his hand slipped under my dress. I fought not to check out in my mind. My front door slammed shut and Allen reached for his gun while pinning me down with his body. Liam came charging towards him and he pulled the trigger. The loud gunshot made me cover my ears and I screamed. Liam crashed into Allen which knocked him off of me. I scrambled up off the floor and breathed a sigh of relief. There was Liam on top of Allen beating the shit out of him. When Liam pulled at some device on his key ring and wrapped a wire around Allen's neck, I knew I had to intercede before he killed him. Allen struggled under Liam's hold. His eyes bucked open and the color was draining from his face.

"Liam! Liam stop it! You're going to kill him!" I rushed to his side and gently placed my hands on his back. Liam tensed but he loosened his grip and push an unconscious Allen over on the floor. His murderous gaze remained focused on Allen.

"I need you to look at me. It's okay. You're here. We're safe now." Liam stood up and took several deep breaths to tame the beast within. He then turned to me. He held my face as he took a visual scan of me from head to toe.

"Are you okay? Did he…?"

"Yes, I'm okay and no. Liam you're bleeding. Oh my God he shot you." I ran for my phone and dialed 9-1-1 before I ran upstairs to get Sade. I assured her that everything was okay and made her stay in her room. When I got back downstairs Liam sat against the wall holding his arm. I ran to the closet and grabbed towels and a first aid kit.

"The ambulance is on the way. I used the towel to apply pressure to his wound to stop the bleeding. My hands trembled and Liam's landed on top of mine.

"Hey. I'm going to be okay." I sniffled and nodded my head. The police arrived before the EMTs. Allen was handcuffed and place in the cop car. When the EMTs came I followed Liam outside and into the ambulance.

"I can't ride with you. I don't want Sade to know that you are hurt. I'm going to take her to Nika's, and I will meet you at the hospital."

I leaned down and kissed his lips. He blinked a few times before his fluttered eyes closed.

"Liam. Liam! What's wrong with him?" I screamed.

"Ma'am we need to get him to the hospital asap."

CHAPTER TWENTY-THREE

Liam

"**C**an I get you anything else, Baby?"

"No, Ray, I'm fine. The only thing I need from you is to get your fine ass up in this bed with me. Especially if you insist on me being in it when I am completely fine."

"You were shot." Her tone was clipped.

"And it was not the first time. My shoulder hurts like hell but I am fine. You and your sisters have done enough." My tone dripped with sarcasm.

After passing out from blood loss, I woke up in the hospital with a gunshot wound to the shoulder. The last thing I remembered was beating Allen's ass and that shit felt good. What I really wanted to do was to take his head completely off. I underwent surgery to get the bullet out and would need to continue with physical therapy to increase mobility in my shoulder. Triple R had insisted that I recover back at the estate. Raven had finally mustered up the courage to return to her childhood home. They were in the process of remodeling the other wing in preparation of opening their own bed and breakfast. Raven had been providing around the clock care and I needed her to rest; she hadn't left my side. Besides taking care of me she still had Sade to look after who was doing virtual school and she was overseeing the designs for the B and B. Raven's bottom lip trembled and I softened my expression.

"Come here." She finally gave in and climbed in the bed with me. I flinched as I shifted my body to get comfortable. Once I had her secured in my arms, she released a shaky breath.

"The end of that night could have been much worse. I could have lost you, Liam. My daughter was right upstairs. When you passed out, I thought I was going to lose you," she whispered into my chest.

"I'm military built. It's going to take a lot more to get rid of me. Nothing was going to happen to the two of you."

"Are you sure they didn't perform any secret experiments on you? Made you into some indestructible, mortal, fighting, killing machine? You know I've always wanted my own terminator."

"Shut up Ray." We both laughed and she snuggled up closer. I rubbed my hand up and down her arm then down her body until I gripped her ass. "You know what I really want?"

"Nope, not that. You need your strength to get better."

"Nah, I got the strength of ten horses." I pulled Raven on top of me so that she could feel just how bad I wanted her. She flashed a devious smile and released me from my sweats. Her soft hand squeezed me with just the right amount of pressure as she worked her hand up and down my shaft. My head fell back when her mouth made contact.

"Fuck Ray. Just like that baby."

"Hey guys we were going to order... Oh shit! I am so sorry. Got damn!"

"Rayne! Get out!" Raven jumped up and pushed her sister out of the room before shutting and locking the door. She flashed an amused smile and began to shed herself of her clothes.

"Now, where were we?"

We finally came up for air in time to get ready for dinner. For the bed and breakfast, we set up outside dining with a huge wooden table. There were strategically placed solar lights and candles on the table. It had a view of the garden and the lake. I made sure to sit facing the garden. Everyone was there, Rasheeda and Hakeem, Leith, Rayne, who's fiancé was conveniently missing, the kids, and Nelson, Rah and Raynnie's dad. We feasted on tacos and margaritas. Liam and I kissed and touched in between eating and drinking.

"You guys are just so stinking cute. It makes me sick." Rayne's brow furrowed but she eventually broke character and smiled. She used her knife to point at Liam.

"You make my sister very happy Liam. Don't screw it up or you will have two protective big sisters and Rah's gang banging husband coming at your neck."

"Damn, I'm getting threatened. I thought we were cool Rayne."

"And let *my* past stay in the past!" Hakeem yelled across the table. Rayne stuck her tongue out at him. Leith leaned towards Rayne and said something in her ear that had her rolling her eyes and scooting away from him.

"Obviously I am all about team Liam, but that's my baby sister. I'm happy for the both of you."

"Thanks sissy."

"Now if Liam can just convince your ass that marriage is not a restriction. Ouch!" Yeah, I kicked her ass under the table. Liam had no idea about my views when it came to marriage. I was all for commitment, but I never understood why marriage was necessary. Well, not until recently. Liam stopped mid sip with his glass hovering in his hand. He looked over at me and raised an eyebrow. He hated not knowing things about me.

"Take a walk with me." He pushed away from the table and held his hand out for me. I placed my hands in his and followed.

I could hear the faint conversation and jokes about me being in trouble. Liam led me to the garden then under the gazebo. His thumb rubbed the inside of my wrist. When our eyes met, I bit my bottom lip.

"You don't want to get married?"

"Do you?"

"Baby I asked you first." Liam sighed and pinched the bridge of his nose.

"I don't know. If you would have asked me this a year ago I would have said no, but now..." I shrugged my shoulders. I moved closer and interlocked my fingers with his. "You make me reconsider."

"I want you to be my wife Raven." Never one to beat around the bush his gaze was intense and searing. As he kneeled down, he reached inside his pocket.

"Hell yes!"

"Damn Raven!"

"What? I know you love me." Liam didn't have to give me a lengthy speech about how much he was in love with me because he showed me with every interaction. I felt and lived in his love every single day. If he wanted marriage, then I was game. He flashed me a devilish grin then slipped the vintage style opal ring on to my finger. The stone was round, surrounded by diamonds on a rose gold band. It was perfect.

"Marriage and family have never been in my future, but I have never been surer that I want it with you. I want to wake up to you every morning. I want to come home to your shoes by the door and your sweaters and blankets all over the house; teach Sade new things. Never do I want to go a day without hearing you laugh and snort. I was made to be the calm to your storm as you are mine in unimaginable ways. You mentioned that you wanted love like what you read about in those romance books that you love so much. I will love you like that. I want forever with you Raven."

His touching words brought tears to my eyes. I raised up on the balls of my feet and wrapped my arms around his neck.

His lips pressed into mine and our tongues tangled in a sensual dance.

"Liam baby you got it."

Epilogue

Two years later.

We struggled with getting pregnant. Struggled with getting pregnant and I struggled with carrying to term. After two miscarriages I was heartbroken and angry. No matter how much of a bitch I grew into Liam never wavered; he never left myside. To him I was the best thing since streaming services, but I put him through the ringer. I fell into a depression after the last miscarriage and vowed that I was done trying but my husband wasn't having it. He refused to have long periods where we weren't connecting physically or at all for that matter. Leading up Valentine's day he planned seven days of sexy romantic dates, all of which ended with him sexing me like crazy. Six weeks later I found myself rushing out of one of my classes to puke my brains out. A positive pregnancy test revealed what I knew would be our rainbow baby. After I got over the morning sickness it was such an easy pregnancy. I guess it was too much to expect an easy labor and delivery.

Baby Washington wasn't due for three weeks, so we decided to take a trip up to the cabin. To Liam's surprise I wanted our time together to be quiet and secluded. I'd grown to appreciate those moments more. A few hours after we'd gotten to the house, I begin to cramp but I chucked it up to Braxton Hick's contractions. Two hours later I was on my knees crawling to find Liam. The back-to-back contractions were doing karate on my uterus and had me unable to walk. Liam lost his shit when he found me on the floor. We called the doctor and she instructed that he get me to the hospital immediately. Liam lifted me into his arms and the feeling of something between my legs caused me to panic.

"No! No, no, no. Wait Liam. Something's there. Something is there. Oh my God! Put me down!" I yelled and panted.

"Ray stop. I need to get you to the hospital." Liam gritted while he struggled to hold his flailing wife in his arms.

"No put me down. I can't hold it I need to push. Got dammit Liam put me down!" I don't know if it was the bass in my voice or the fear in my eyes, but Liam rushed to put me down on bed. Frantically, I began ripping at my clothes. My t-shirt was flung across the room. I was hot. Next, I tried to pull my pants down. I yanked and tugged like a crazy person until Liam pull them down the rest of the way and my legs flew open.

"Oh, shit, Ray. The baby."

"WHAT? What's wrong." Tears spilled down my face.

"Nah suck that shit up baby because I need you to push."

"Wh- what!"

"Fuckin' push Raven!"

When I felt my next contraction, I tucked my chin into my chest and pushed with all the strength that I had. It felt like my kitty was being ripped apart. Liam was never touching me again. My hands clenched the sheets, and I screamed my released. Then, just like, that the pain was gone, and I instantly felt relief. A strong cry filled the room and I bawled. Tears clouded my vision. I needed to see my baby.

"Baby you did it!" Liam was at my side wiping my tears. His movements were minimal due to the umbilical cord still being attached to the baby.

"What's its name?" We had decided that we wanted to wait to find out the gender. My doctor was provided with the names we had chosen if it was a boy or girl. The plan was for her to announce the gender by introducing our baby by his or her name.

"Raven, meet Levi Jackson Washington." Upon hearing the tremble and emotion in his voice, I looked up at him. Tears ran down his face. He stared down at our son, enamored. The only times that I've seen him emotional like this was when my father died and on our wedding day. He leaned down and kissed me on the lips. My heart swelled.

"A boy?"

"Yes." He carefully laid Levi on my bare chest.

After a few hours and a visit from my doctor. I sat up in the bed gazing upon my son in complete awe. My sisters had stopped by and dropped Sade off. They were excited to love on the first boy of the family, but they gave us our privacy. My oldest sat on my right with her head resting on my shoulder as she held her brother's hand. He was beautiful. He looked everything like his damn daddy, and I couldn't be happier. Levi was huge like his daddy too. He weighed in at nine pounds, thirteen ounces and twenty-two inches long. My poor kitty. I hummed Twinkle, Twinkle Little Star and Sade joined in. It was the song my mom sang to me and I sang to Sade. Liam stood in the door frame, shirtless, and watched his family. I gave him an appreciative once over. His eyes held so much contentment and pride. Liam was emotional and keeping his distance; he could only handle so much emotion at once.

"I need you closer Liam." I hummed. He visibly relaxed then joined me on my left. When he reached for Levi I obliged. He carefully laid him on his bare chest and stroked his head.

"How are you feeling?" He spoke lowly.

"Like I ran a marathon through hell with gasoline drawers on, but my prize was another little piece of heaven." I looked over to catch his serious expression.

"Mom, your words," Sade warned. She snuggled up closer to me and hadn't left my side since she arrived.

"Seriously, Ray."

"I'm good. Better now that my family is all here. What about you, Daddy?" Liam grinned at his new title and looked over at Sade and me.

"I feel blessed and whole. I feel loved. I couldn't ask for anything more. Thank you for not giving up on me. Thank you for seeing *me*. Thank you for my family, Ray."

"Please, don't thank me. I needed to make sure that you never tried to run away from me again. Had to lock you down permanently. The ring was a start, but I needed extra insurance." I winked.

"Baby I'm serious."

I smirked and interlaced my hand with his. "I know. Thank you for loving me right and allowing me to be me. Thank you for making me and Sade feel loved, safe, and secure. Thank you for loving Sade and forming your own special relationship with her. You make me want to be a better person. You're also fine as hell and I needed to lock you down."

It was funny how God put together two complete opposites. One who was running towards love and the other who did nothing but run from it, but we found the love we required in each other and found our way. There was no doubt in my mind that this was forever. Liam laughed and kissed me in a way that had me blushing in front of my children.

"I love y'all."

Sade and I responded in unison. "We love you too."

I couldn't have asked for a better love than this.

The End.

ABOUT THE AUTHOR

Takisha Trenean

Born and raised in Miami, Florida, TaKisha Trenean is both a writer and an avid reader. TaKisha has always had a passion for writing and enjoys giving life to characters through penning romantic stories showcasing black love. Throughout her formative years she would journal and write poetry as a form expressing herself and documenting her experiences. Writing romance gives life to the hopeless romantic within her and allows the introvert within to explore life through her characters. Inspired by music and the world around her, TaKisha hopes to create stories that readers can ultimately relate to and get lost in.

TaKisha Trenean resides in Miami, Florida where she provides success coaching to former foster youth. Aside from writing she enjoys spending her days wrapped up in a good book or binge watching her favorite TV shows.

BOOKS BY TAKISHA TRENEAN

For The Love of You: A Miami Street King Novel

For The Love of You 2: A Miami Street King Novel

Love Will Never Do Without You

Kindred Hearts

Seasons of Love: A Kindred Hearts Novella

Love Captured

Love Awakened

Don't Waste My Time

Love Me Like That

Her Christmas Secret

CONNECT WITH
TAKISHA TRENEAN

Facebook: @takishatrenean
https://www.facebook.com/takisha.trenean.92

Instagram: @takisha_trenean
https://www.instagram.com/takisha_trenean/

Amazon: amazon.com/author/takishatrenean